A DONKEY'S FOR THE KING

ALSO BY JOHN AND PATRICIA BEATTY

At the Seven Stars (1963)
Campion Towers (1965)

BY PATRICIA BEATTY

Indian Canoemaker (1960)
Bonanza Girl (1962)
The Nickel-Plated Beauty (1964)

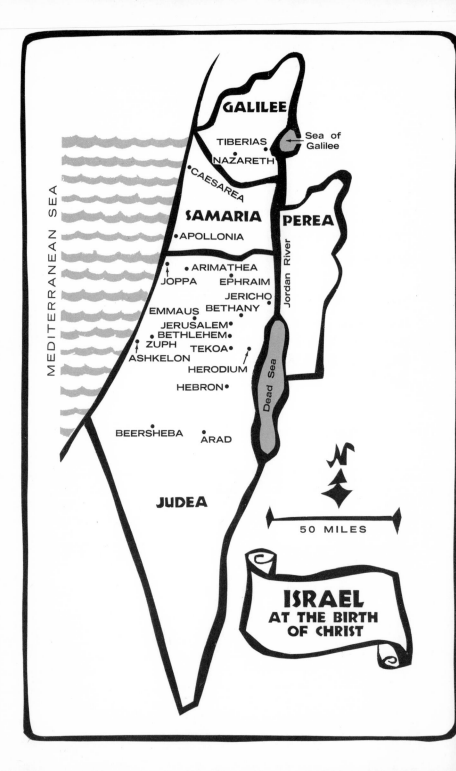

A DONKEY FOR THE KING

JOHN AND PATRICIA BEATTY

WOODCUTS BY ANNE SIBERELL

THE MACMILLAN COMPANY, NEW YORK

THE MACMILLAN COMPANY, NEW YORK
COLLIER-MACMILLAN CANADA, LTD., TORONTO, ONTARIO
LIBRARY OF CONGRESS CATALOG CARD NUMBER: 66–18200
PRINTED IN THE UNITED STATES OF AMERICA
FIRST PRINTING

FOR

Peggy Hampton

AND FOR

Marian Jeffrey
Alice Bridges
Grace Shirley
Nancy Krause

CONTENTS

I. THE SON OF ABDIEL

With a deep sigh, one so deep that the ewe nearest him looked around to see, Jesse, son of Abdiel, put down his shepherd's flute.

He sighed often now as he thought of his father, Abdiel, who lay ill in his Uncle Habor's house on sleeping mats like a man already dead. He sighed, too, when he thought of his Uncle Habor, his father's only brother.

There was trouble in Habor's house in the village of Arad, and it was not only because of Abdiel, who had not been able to work in Habor's carpenter

1

shop since the summer month of Tammuz, ten months past. It was because of Habor's wife, the woman Habor had found in northern Judea, married, and brought to southern Judea—to Arad.

Jesse sat in the warm sun of the month of Ilyan, his back against a great rock, his ironbound cudgel beside him and Habor's old brown sheep dog at his feet, her ears pricked forward in case a thieving lion or wolf came out of the hills nearby to steal a lamb or if an eagle dropped from the sky. Habor's sheep grazed on the hillside below Jesse and Tob, the dog. Now and then a ewe lifted her head to bleat while the afternoon drained itself slowly away.

The boy sighed once more and wiped his forehead with his sleeve. He took off his *piljon,* his skullcap, and ran a cloth over his face. Then he got up and drank from the goatskin of water slung across his chest. His brown, black and gray striped robe was tattered, its tasseled edges frayed, and his linen tunic beneath it was soiled and torn. His long black hair was a tangled mat of wet curls. Large dark eyes blazed out of his sun-darkened face.

The sun was halfway down in the western sky and already purple clouds flecked the horizon behind the hills. It was time to take the flock to the sheepfold behind Habor's house. Unlike many other shepherds, Habor did not leave his sheep in the hills from the time of the Passover to the end of autumn. Jesse was not yet a man—he could not remain for six months with the flocks. He would have to hurry if he was to get to Arad before nightfall. And there was another cause to hurry, too. Habor's wife became very angry when anyone was late to the evening meal—almost as angry as when a boy of twelve ate too much. Jesse knew that his aunt believed he was greedy, and he tried to control his appetite so she wouldn't scowl at him. He did this for his father's sake. Jesse made a low growling sound in his throat—the only sound he could make, for the son of Abdiel was a mute. But brown, shaggy Tob understood what this meant. The boy touched her with his hand and pointed. As Jesse moved out with his shepherd's pipes to lead the flock down the hillside, Tob darted away to bark and snap at the heels of Habor's ewes and lambs.

The boy did not once look back to see how Tob fared. He knew that Tob was as fine a sheep dog as Jesse was a shepherd. The boy and dog got on very well, although Tob, like everything else, did not belong to Jesse. She was Habor's dog and was despised by Habor's wife, but that was not too strange, for dogs were generally despised in Israel as scavengers. But Jesse liked Tob. He loved all animals—even dogs.

Followed by the sheep, freshly shorn that month, Jesse went along, playing a melancholy tune that he had composed himself. He would pipe as he took Habor's sheep through Arad. That way the people of the village would take notice that although Jesse ben Abdiel was a mute, he could play a tune as well as any shepherd boy in Israel—if not better. The boy loved music and his pipes. Outside of his father, and Tob, his shepherd's pipes were his only friends.

The son of Abdiel knew all too well how the people of Arad felt about him and about his father, who could speak of only one thing, the coming of the Messiah. The folk of Arad hated Abdiel and Jesse, who were strange ones—although both had lived all their lives in the village. A fire burned in the deep-set eyes of father and son. The boy, whose mother had died soon after he was born, had been struck by a terrible fever when he was six years old and since that time had not been able to speak a word.

The boy was silent, always silent. Not so the father. He was a nuisance. He would speak of one thing only. Abdiel believed that the Messiah would soon come to Israel. This was his constant and sole refrain. Men had once argued with him, but as Abdiel's obsession grew, they avoided him and his singleminded conversation to keep the peace. The people of Arad had given up hoping for the Messiah. Israel had waited too long! Even the rabbi of Arad no longer accepted what the prophets of Israel had said so long ago about the coming of the "promised one." Before Abdiel had become bedridden with his illness, though, his mania had grown far worse. He had had visions and seen signs and omens in the skies. He had rushed about southern Judea preaching wildly to strangers—to anyone who would listen, even lepers and beggars—about the coming of the savior of Israel, the coming of the man who would tear away the yoke of Rome and of King Herod. For this was what was prophesied of the man "who was to come" and to be crowned King of the Jews.

No one had reported Abdiel to King Herod, who was far away to the north in his palace in Jerusalem. Fanatics and madmen were common in Judea. They were almost as common as robbers on the roads, and they were generally avoided. Men who preached of the Messiah were not really very dangerous. They were laughable more than anything else, and they could be bores. There were always such men about in the land. Mighty Herod would probably not take notice of a humble carpenter from Arad who said very loudly that the Messiah would topple him from his throne. However, one could never tell about Herod. Still and all, Habor worried. His wife told him that he should.

Habor was that sort of man. She was that sort of woman.

Habor locked Abdiel, his younger brother, up in his house—half to save Habor's family from more embarrassment in Arad, half to keep Abdiel from saying anything more about Herod, whose eyes and ears could be anywhere in Israel.

The Romans, the awesome Romans, did not overly concern Habor. Although the emperor of Rome was the real ruler of Israel, Caesar Augustus had never once come to Arad, and his soldiers had come marching through only once in Habor's lifetime. The people of Arad did not often think of Rome, except to shudder and complain about the high taxes they had to pay. But they *did* consider King Herod.

After Habor had locked Abdiel in an upper room, Abdiel had soon become very weak and had taken to his bed. Jesse knew this was because his father had no one to talk to about the Messiah any more. And there was no one in Arad to help Abdiel. Not even the rabbi could. He had come to reason with Habor, but Habor's wife had met him at the door of her house, her arms folded and a harsh expression on her face. Wisely the rabbi had retreated.

Jesse, sitting alone in a corner of Habor's little courtyard, had seen all this take place. He knew how the woman resented him and his father—now that Abdiel could no longer work. The fact that Jesse was such a good shepherd and had never lost a lamb did not make her tolerate him any better. The boy knew in his heart why she disliked him so—because he was a mute, because there was something "wrong" with him. There was nothing wrong with her three daughters—all were comely and any one of them could out-argue any other woman of Arad at the village well. Habor's wife had no use for talk of the Messiah. As long as bread was baked, her house was kept in good order, her neighbor's activities were gossip-worthy, and Habor's carpenter shop flourished, she was content. Or rather she would have been content with two less mouths to feed.

As he led the sheep into Arad, Jesse thought bitterly of her and of his father and then fleetingly about the Messiah. He did not know what he believed about the "man who was to come." His father said one thing, but the rabbi and Habor said another. What was a boy to think? Perhaps the best thing was not to think at all about something that lay so far ahead in the future—if his "coming" was a real promise at all. It was difficult to tell exactly what the old prophets had meant. They had spoken so vaguely and strangely. The health of his father should concern Jesse most—not the Messiah. Generations of people in Israel had lived and died waiting for the Messiah to make his appearance. And the "promised one" was yet to come!

The boy went through the dusty village, and once he had put the bawling sheep in Habor's fold, he went into his uncle's courtyard. Jesse was hungry again. The barley bread and goat's-milk cheese his aunt had sent him out with at dawn had not filled up even one leg. He hoped he would not disgrace himself and his father again by eating too much at the evening meal.

Anna, Habor's second daughter, the kindest one, spoke to Jesse. She was seated under the olive tree carding wool, and she looked up from her work as he went by. She resembled her mother, plump and brown-eyed. "Go, see your father, Jesse," she told him. "He has had a bad day."

Jesse nodded his head. Then he brushed the dust from his robe before he put his hand to his lips and touched the *mezuzah*, the written word of God sealed in a leather container on the doorpost, and entered his uncle's house. He climbed the outside steps that led to Habor's upper story, his heart thudding with fear at what he might find.

Abdiel had once been a tall, bronze-skinned, black-bearded man. Now he was shrunken and his beard was streaked with gray. His complexion was yellowish, his breathing hard. With his eyes closed, his hands on his chest, he lay on the floor on soft thick mats.

Habor, who looked much as Abdiel had before his illness, sat above him on a stool, his dark robe caught about him as if he had a chill. Over his shoulders he wore his *tallith*, his prayer shawl. Habor had been praying for his brother. The tiny bare-walled room was cold. No charcoal brazier warmed it, and the rays of the setting sun held no heat.

Habor was silent for a moment as he looked at the boy, who did not kiss his uncle as usual. Then the man spoke. "Abdiel has not said a word to us all this day. The rabbi came to visit him, but Abdiel did not seem to know him. He opened his eyes only once when the rabbi called to him. I saw Abdiel look at him as if he had never seen him before. Then, your father shook his head twice. After that . . ." Habor's voice trailed off as he gestured helplessly with his hands. "Here! You sit with him for a time, Jesse. Perhaps he will know you." Habor got up from his stool and the boy took his place.

Jesse picked up his father's hand, kissed it, and squeezed it twice. The squeeze was a signal between them that Jesse wished Abdiel to speak to him. Often, though, father and son communicated by thoughts passing from one to the other. The people of Arad found this ability eerie and frightening. They preferred noisy chattering at the village well and at the shops. Abdiel himself could not read or write, but he had seen to it that Jesse knew a few letters, learned from the rabbi. It was not possible that Jesse could be a scribe, of course. To be a scribe required speech, Abdiel thought. But from that day long ago when the disease had struck at the boy's throat, Abdiel had worried what was to become of his son. He had felt that Jesse would be better suited for life if he could read and write a little. Jesse sometimes wished he knew more and that Habor and his wife would permit him more time with the rabbi. He liked the rabbi of Arad, but his uncle's sheep had needed a shepherd, and Abdiel, who had been unable to work for ten months, brought in no money.

Once more the mute boy squeezed his father's hand. This time Abdiel opened his eyes, but he did not smile. His lips moved. Jesse's hearing was very acute, so acute that some of the people of Arad believed he could hear through walls, but he had to bend his head to hear his father speak.

"The Messiah," Abdiel whispered. "I have dreamed that he comes, and soon—very soon!"

Jesse nodded. His father had spoken to him always of the Messiah. In his illness he spoke of no one else. Abdiel was more than ever obsessed with the Messiah now.

Putting his hands over his son's, Abdiel sighed weakly. "Very soon, very soon, my son. *You* will know him!"

Once again the boy bobbed his head to let his father know he had understood and then sat for a time with Abdiel, who had fallen back into sleep after he had spoken.

During the evening meal Habor was with the

boy's father. Jesse saw him but for a brief moment to say good night and to murmur a prayer over him, but this time his father did not speak to him.

During the night *Malach Hamavet*, the angel of death, came to the house of Habor, the carpenter, and took Abdiel with him.

Habor went to Jesse early in the morning and awoke him where he slept on his mat in the little shed behind the house. Tears shone in Habor's eyes. "It is finished, Jesse," he told the boy. "Your father is dead. The women of Arad attend to him now, and a cave is being prepared in the hills to receive him."

Jesse put his face in his robe, but he did not weep. Jesse had never wept that anyone could remember, not even when he was hurt as a small child. The people of Arad believed that because he was a mute he could not weep. But they were very wrong. The son of Abdiel would not give way to emotion before his father's enemies. He did not weep in the days that passed, although Habor's house was filled with paid women mourners who wailed and tore their garments with grief. He did not weep even when his father's body was carried from the house and put in one of the many caves that honeycombed the hills, nor did he weep at the funeral feast.

Ten days after the death of his father, Habor called to Jesse to come to him in the evening after the boy had returned to Arad with the sheep. Habor sat at his table. His wife stood near him stirring the kettle that held the night's supper of onions and lentils.

Habor was embarrassed. He looked at his hands while he spoke to his nephew. "We must speak now about your future, Jesse," he said too loudly.

Jesse stood motionless. What would Habor say next? He had noticed out of the corner of his eye that Habor's wife had turned her broad back to him.

"Your father had nothing to leave you," Habor went on. "What little he had went long ago to buy medicines in his illness."

Without turning around, Jesse's aunt broke in, "Habor borrowed silver to bring that physician *all* the way from Jerusalem, and what good did he do for your father, I ask you? Rather we should have sent for a wandering rabbi, one who drives out devils. We must repay that silver yet to the money-lender."

"That is true," Habor agreed with his wife, "and we are poorer than we were before."

"A good deal poorer," added the woman. She paused for a moment, then went on more briskly, her voice hardening. "Our daughters are almost of marriageable age. Anna's cousin from Beersheba

has asked for her. He will give the fifty shekels
for her, but she must have a bride gift from us.
We must save money for her bride gift and for my
other daughters."

"Anna's husband-to-be is also a shepherd, Jesse."
Habor now fidgeted with the sleeves of his robe.
"He will put his sheep with my flock when he and
Anna wed."

"We will not need you any more, Jesse. We are
sending you to my cousin Nabal." It was Habor's
wife who said the cruel words Jesse had already
guessed he had been called in to hear.

"You will like Nabal," Habor said lamely. "He
owns a circus, a very fine circus."

"My cousin Nabal can always use helpers," the
woman said, tasting the lentil broth. "He once told
me that very thing. He is a very rich man. You will
leave in the morning, Jesse."

"We will give you a little money." Habor looked
at the boy standing before him and tried to smile.
"You will find Nabal north of Jerusalem at this time
of the year, I believe. Ask anyone anywhere near
the city—they all know Nabal and his circus around
Jerusalem." Habor glanced quickly at his wife. "You
will take a letter to Nabal. The rabbi will write it."

"Yes, indeed, they do know my cousin Nabal,"
said the woman, stirring more slowly now. "Nabal
is a very famous man."

"You may have some real adventures traveling

about with such a man," went on Habor. "I always wanted to go with a circus when I was a boy."

He would have said more, but Jesse would not hear it. He turned on his heel and left his uncle's house for the hillside behind it. How he wished he could speak to his uncle's wife, saying the words, "Cursed be your mother!" At this moment he hated his muteness more than he had ever hated it before.

At dawn the next day, washed and dressed in his robe, his prayer shawl, and sandals, Jesse said his prayers, ate what Anna gave him and went to the rabbi's house for the letter to Nabal. Then he came back to bid farewell to Habor and his family. Anna wept openly, and so did one of her other sisters, but Jesse's aunt did not.

Habor gave the boy Abdiel's worn old leather pouch. He dropped some coins into it before Jesse's eyes and then filled it with bread and cheese. Anna gave Jesse Abdiel's wool robe to put over his shoulder. It was to serve as a coverlet on his journey.

"We do not send you out empty-handed, Jesse," Habor told the boy, trying his best to sound hearty. "The pouch your father left you was empty, but I have filled it to the top."

Jesse took it from him and a dry empty gourd for water, never moving his eyes from his uncle's face, which fell under the boy's harsh accusing gaze. Then Jesse left his uncle's courtyard forever. As he passed out of Habor's courtyard, the boy spat once without turning about. Now Habor and his family would understand how the son of Abdiel felt.

Tob followed Jesse to the gate of Habor's house until Habor's wife called to her to come back. The dog obeyed her and returned, tail between her legs. Yet Tob whimpered and her eyes followed Jesse ben Abdiel as far as she could see him as he walked down the street of Arad.

The boy left his village, head high, his staff in his hand, his shepherd's pipes in the bosom of his robe and his dagger at his belt. These, at least, belonged to him, gifts from his father in happier times. A few early risers saw him, but he looked neither to the right nor to the left. No one jeered at him, and he caught one fierce murmur about the "woman" Habor had brought from the north, the woman who turned out her own nephew to starve— but the boy paid no heed to that. He had had enough of Arad. He would never return to it, and as he went by the last house he spat once more.

When he had crossed the last hillside that gave him a glimpse of his father's home, though, Jesse sat on a stone for a time, his head in his hands. Still he did not truly weep, although tears came to his eyes. After a while he got up and started his journey to the north—to Jerusalem.

He put Habor and his family out of his mind

as he walked. Instead he thought of Tob. He would have liked the dog to have been at his side, but now he was alone. Perhaps someday he would have someone of his own who loved him and whom he could love—someone who would travel with him wherever he went—some animal. Of what use were people to the son of Abdiel? They cast him out. He would cast them out.

II. SAUL

For almost a week Jesse walked along the roads of dry tawny Judea. From high ground he sometimes saw the blue waters of the Dead Sea far away across the land on his right. When he saw it and could gaze at its beautiful color, he would sit down to rest and try to repair his sandals, which mile by mile became more and more ragged while his feet became ever sorer. He walked slowly—quite slowly. He was not very eager to find Nabal, famous though he might be.

People on horseback, on donkeyback and afoot

17

passed him on their way north. They paid little attention to the thin, ragged, bitter-faced lad. There were thousands like him in Israel. An old man with a gray beard fell in with Jesse for a time, but when he learned that the boy could not speak with him to while away the miles, the old man left him at a wayside spring.

Only one other traveled with him and spoke to him, a Nazarite, a huge man whose hair and beard had never been cut and who wore a robe of animal skins.

The Nazarite spent a Sabbath with the mute boy, sitting in a grove of terebinths. The Law of Israel did not permit them to travel more than one mile on that day, and Jesse lay on the ground, sharing the Nazarite's food with him—bread as coarse as his own and dried figs. Nazarites, men dedicated from birth to the service of the Eternal, were not rich men, nor did they drink wine.

It had not taken the Nazarite long to learn that Jesse was a mute when he met him at a wayside spring. It did not seem to bother the man. He had found someone to preach to—someone who would not dispute the Torah or the finer points of the Law with him. Jesse's age was no barrier to this—as a twelve-year-old, Jesse ben Abdiel knew the Law.

The Nazarite talked on and on through the fragrant night while the boy half listened. Tonight Jesse's thoughts were back in Arad with Tob and with the flock he had tended. Had a hyena carried off one of the spring lambs? There had been rumors of hyenas skulking about before Jesse had been sent away from Arad. Would the new shepherd, Anna's bridegroom, keep as close watch over the ewes and lambs as he, Jesse, had done? And what of Tob? How was she? Did she like her new master? What would happen to her? Jesse knew that Anna's husband would soon take Anna away with him to Beersheba as was the custom. He would put his sheep with Habor's and then would probably take Habor's flock and his bride with him to the pastures near Beersheba. Would the bridegroom take Tob with him too? If there was no work for the old dog, Habor's wife would not keep her long. There was no need for a watchdog in tiny Arad, where everyone knew everyone else.

The Nazarite broke in on Jesse's worries by saying, "The rich men of Canaan no longer watch and wait for the Messiah, lad. Zechariah, the prophet, has been dead for five hundred years and still we men of Israel have known no true Messiah. False Messiahs, yes, there have been hundreds of them, but the real 'man who is to come'—no! We are poor folk, you and I, not rich men of Jerusalem. Do you watch for him?"

Jesse shook his head from side to side and looked sour. He didn't want to hear of the Messiah now, but the man went on.

"We know he will be born of the House of David, of the stock of Jesse. Some say he will be warlike and will kill the pagans, the Romans and Greeks who pollute this land. Others say he will be a sacrifice, a sad man who will take on the sorrows of all men. I watch for him still, but I do not blame you for not looking for him, boy. I know what men mean when they say to me, 'When the Messiah comes!' and sneer. They might as well ask me why men don't fly like birds."

The Nazarite now yawned and said his prayers. Then he rolled himself in his cloak and fell asleep under the terebinths. As for Jesse, the boy waited until the moon was high—after midnight. The Sabbath was long past. Jesse ben Abdiel stole away from the grove and out into the moonlit road. He had had enough of "the man who was to come," the man who had driven his father to madness. The Nazarite, too, went to Jerusalem. Jesse meant to travel far ahead of him on that road.

A little south of Hebron, Jesse found a day's work. He could not ask for it but when he stepped in among the workers of the wheat harvest and took the reins of the unruly unmuzzled oxen being driven across the yellow mass of sheaves and got them to pull together better than any of the other drovers could do it, the owner of the fields gave the boy a few copper coins. "Ah, you have a way with beasts, lad," said the delighted man. But he did not ask

Jesse to stay on during the winnowing, when the men tossed the grain into the air with wooden forks to separate the chaff from the wheat.

In Hebron, Jesse bought more bread and cheese and old cloths to bind around his feet to save his sandals. He now carried the sandals. He went very slowly on his way again—this time to Herodium, walking in the pale-yellow early morning and in the late afternoon when it was coolest. He did not play his pipes; his heart was not in music now. He slept by the side of the road, knowing that wild animals, the wolves, lions, and bears of Israel, would probably not molest him so close to where humans traveled.

As for robbers, Jesse did not think much about them at all. What did he have for them to steal?

Between Herodium and Bethlehem Jesse saw his first Romans, a maniple of them, a hundred or more, marching eastward toward the Dead Sea. Their sandals shook the earth as the sun glinted on their helmets and breastplates. In order not to be seen, he hid behind a large boulder at the crossroads. Once they were out of sight, the boy hurried northward as fast as his sore feet could take him away from the choking clouds of dust the Romans had made. Jesse had heard terrible stories about the Romans, who were the real rulers of Israel. He didn't know if they were only wild stories for little children that people in Arad had made up, but he didn't intend to be near enough to Romans again to find out.

Jesse found the towns of northern Judea little different from Arad. The houses were made of the same mud brick or of local stone and were the same white cubes. The same steps went up the outside to the upper story in the finer houses. Sometimes he saw tents on the roof and once or twice balconies where the women sat. The people of Hebron, Herodium and Bethlehem were much like the folk of Arad. They dressed the same. The men wore striped woolen robes of brown, black, white and blue over long linen gowns and the *piljon*. Their hair was like Jesse's with long curls over the ears. The women wore colored gowns and over their heads veils to cover their hair. The women of these towns that Jesse passed through were kind to the boy as they drew water from the village wells. They knew what he wanted when he sat on the well's edge to rest. They gave him water to drink from their pitchers and refilled his gourd. They never knew he was a mute. Men did not speak to Jewish women they did not know. It was the custom in Israel. But all the same they smiled at the thin, hot-eyed boy. He often longed to be able to ask them for a bed at night. But how could he do this, even though it was the custom of travelers, when he could not speak to them? And the little money Habor had given his nephew would not permit

him to buy even a corner in a wayside inn if he
was to make his way to Jerusalem without starving.

Jesse kept the letter the rabbi had written for
him to give Nabal inside his robe above his shepherd's dagger and pipes. Once he'd looked at it
while he rested, but he could make out only a few
of the words—his name, Nabal's, and one or two
others. The rabbi had written it in handsome
Hebrew letters. How wonderful it must be to be
able to do such a thing, Jesse thought!

It didn't occur to him to do anything but to go
to Nabal, the circus owner. There was nothing
behind for Jesse, the son of mad, demon-possessed
Abdiel, in Arad. His future lay somewhere north
of Jerusalem—wherever Nabal traveled now. Jesse
could write Nabal's name and the word for "circus."
The gentle, far-seeing rabbi had taught him those
particular words, but the boy did not intend to
use them until he came to Jerusalem. Why try to
find a circus south of that city when it was supposed
to be in the north? The boy trusted the information
Habor's wife had given him. She was never wrong
—about matters that concerned her purse.

Seven days after he left Arad, Jesse stood among
the olive groves in the hills before the walls of
Jerusalem, the "city of the high place." He heard
the blasts of the seven silver trumpets ringing out
over the city, trumpets being blown in the great

temple whose gilded spires rose high over the wall.
The sound made him shiver and think for a moment
of his father. Abdiel had gone to Jerusalem to the
temple to sacrifice more than once, but he had not
taken Jesse with him—not since the boy had gone
there as a baby twelve years past to fulfill the Law
of Israel, which said newborn babies must be
brought to the temple. As the last note fell into
nothingness, the boy thought once again of the
Messiah, the man who was "to come" to be King
of the Jews. But Jesse's thought was only a swiftly
passing one. The rabbi had spoken to him very seriously of the Messiah after Abdiel's death, telling
him that Abdiel's obsession was a foolish one and
that Jesse would be wise not to share it. Watching
for the Messiah was the pastime of fools and old
women. The Nazarite he'd met on the road had
only upset the boy further. Now the son of Abdiel
decided that he would pattern himself on the wiser,
richer men of his land and deny that any Messiah
would ever come.

The boy had admired walled Jerusalem from a
hill to its south, seeing it as the first rays of sun
turned its ochre buildings to deep gold and its white
palaces to deep yellow. Jesse didn't choose to enter
it—the city of David and Solomon, the holy city
of the Israelites for ten centuries—unless he must.
He admired it and feared it. It was so large—far
larger than he had dreamed it could be. No, he

would seek at the gates for news of Nabal, the circus owner.

With a camel caravan carrying incense from Arabia for the great temple, and with horse and slave dealers, all with goods to sell, Jesse made his way to the great gate on the west of the city, the Gate of Ephraim. Awestruck by its size, he gazed up at it. Its wide stone towers rose high into the air and a wide road went between them. He watched the men and animals passing into the city and saw travelers on donkeyback coming out. A Roman messenger sped away over the stones in a chariot as the boy looked after him. How the Roman glittered in his breastplate and helmet! How his scarlet cloak and horsehair plume danced in the breeze as he swung his whip out over his fine white horse!

And what fabulous people the boy from Arad saw. A group of Phoenician merchants rode slowly into Jerusalem, their tunics gay with color above their striped trousers. Not far behind them came a Persian nobleman with a crowd of servants preceding and following him. One of them held a great blue umbrella over his master's head to shield him and his wonderful yellow, purple and gold brocade gown from the sun that had risen only a short time before. The sweet odor of perfume came floating to Jesse's nose as a lady in flowing robes of pale green came out on donkeyback. He sniffed greedily at the scent of jasmine and cassia, and the lady smiled at him with reddened lips and looked at him from eyes darkened with antimony. Her beribboned hair, piled high on top of her head, had been tinted with Egyptian henna, and the palms of her hands were dyed yellow-red. Jesse ben Abdiel had never seen such a beautiful lady—nor had he seen such stern-looking men as the two black-silk-robed, black-bearded Babylonians who followed her and her servant out of the "city of the high place." To the boy's amazement the Babylonians wore gold rings in their noses.

Jesse waited, patient and more than a little frightened, taking in all of the sights, until there was a quiet space in the traffic.

And then he did not go up to any of the guards, who stood stiffly, their hands on spears, their faces hard-set under helmets. Instead he sought out a man sitting at the bottom of the wall, his feet drawn up, his arms clasped about his knees as if he waited. The man was fat and had a good-natured face, so the boy, although he loathed revealing his muteness, decided he would try to learn from him what he must know.

Jesse squatted before the man and in the dirt wrote Nabal's name.

"Peace be with you," said the stranger. "Why do you write 'Nabal' there, boy? I don't read too well, but I know that name well enough. It was my

brother's. What do you want of me? Can't you
speak?"

Jesse point to his mouth and shook his head, then
put his hand behind his ear and nodded twice to
show he was able to hear.

The man of the wall nodded, too. "I see. You are
dumb, but you can hear and understand. Which
Nabal do you seek? I know half a dozen Nabals in
Jerusalem. What particular Nabal do you have in
mind? Hurry! I am waiting here to join a party of
travelers to Arimathea. This could take all morning,
dealing with you, but I haven't got all morning."

Jesse traced the word "circus," but the stranger
didn't know that word. Then desperately and as
swiftly as he could, the boy drew the figures of
men and then of animals, but still the stranger shook
his head.

"No, I don't know any Nabal who sells animals
in Jerusalem."

Now Jesse rubbed out what he'd done and drew
a lion. Jesse drew well—as a mute he'd had a great
deal of practice.

"A wild-animal dealer? That's a good trade—a
rich one. The Romans buy lions for their circuses
all the time, that's what they tell me in—"

This time the stranger did understand. He
laughed. "*That* one! So that's the Nabal you want—
the well-known one? Well, you won't find him in
Jerusalem. You won't find him here for quite a

while—not after that last unpleasant business. I can't see why you'd want to locate him, but I suppose you must—if you go to all of this trouble."

Jesse nodded once again and pointed north, south, east, and west and then looked inquisitive.

"Emmaus, that's where I heard that scoundrel Nabal betook himself. Go to Emmaus if you must find Nabal, but if you take my advice, you won't even try. You'll go back where you came from—wherever that is."

The man of the wall pointed westward, toward Emmaus.

Jesse gestured a thank you, wished he could say "May heaven be with you" to the stranger who had helped him, then turned his back to the great gate and walked away to the west. He thought of the things the stranger had told him as he went. He'd believed at first that he'd had great good luck learning Nabal's whereabouts so easily, but the other things the man had told him made him uneasy. What was the "well-known" Nabal like? Why couldn't Nabal bring his circus back to Jerusalem?

Emmaus was a two days' walk for Jesse, whose feet were now very sore and bruised. He passed through a greener countryside than he had known before, although he was still in the province of Judea. He saw no circus as he came into Emmaus, and for a good while he hesitated by the well, wondering what he should do. Then he went to the synagogue. The rabbi would help him.

The boy found the rabbi, a sandalmaker, in his house near the small temple, kissed his hand, and gave the letter to him. The rabbi unrolled it and read it swiftly, translating the Hebrew words into Aramaic, the language he and Jesse knew.

"The letter states that you are Jesse, son of Abdiel, and nephew of Habor, both of Arad, and that you are a mute but can hear and understand well enough. Is this so?"

Jesse nodded. Sometimes nodding and shaking his head so much made it ache.

"And you have been sent to find a kinsman of your aunt, a certain Nabal who owns a circus?"

Once more the boy bobbed agreement.

"You will find Nabal at the inn of Gezer at midday. His circus," the rabbi frowned as he said it, "is encamped west of the town. Jesse ben Abdiel," the rabbi asked sharply, "what do you know of this man?"

Jesse shook his head and spread out his hands to show that he knew nothing at all.

The rabbi sighed, "May the Eternal protect you, then," he said.

Jesse found the inn of Gezer easily enough. The rabbi had told him that the *Menorah*, the seven-branched candlestick, was painted on its outer wall, and he had given Jesse a brief letter to Gezer, the innkeeper.

Where the rabbi had been a short thin man, the innkeeper was a tall thin one with small shrewd black eyes. He took the rabbi's letter, read it and jerked with his thumb toward a table where three men sat, drinking and casting dice, playing a game to see who bought the next cups of wine.

"Nabal wears the red-and-black robe," Gezer told the boy as he walked off to serve another customer, a long-haired, beardless young man who spoke loudly of the merits of a rich old widow of Jerusalem, a woman he planned to marry for her wealth.

Jesse went to stand at Nabal's side, waiting until the man should look up at him. Nabal didn't. He reached for the dice instead and threw them onto the table. One of his companions spoke to him finally.

"The brat wants something of ye, Nabal."

"Eh," grunted the man. He now looked at Jesse, one hand reaching toward the dice.

Jesse held the letter from Arad out to his aunt's cousin, who took it and read it with difficulty, his lips moving. Then he gave it back to Jesse, shoving it into his hands.

"Take yourself back to Arad, boy. I've got no use for you. *He's a mute!*" Nabal shouted these words to the men with him. "My cousin, a woman I've seen only once, a woman who is a harridan if ever I've seen one, sends me a mute! Why didn't she send me an acrobat? That's what I need, an acrobat."

"What about a new lion, Nabal? Yours is toothless," said one of the other men, laughing.

"Or a young dancing donkey—as long as I am wishing for the moon—or a big bag of gold from Caesar Augustus, himself, sent posthaste to me from Rome?" Nabal said, wiping his mouth with his sleeve. "Don't tell me my troubles, friends. I know them well enough as it is. Why do you think I come here to drink—to remember how badly things go with me? They have not gone well since I took my circus out of Jerusalem, where there are crowds of citizens and pilgrims coming to the temple who pay well to see my performers." He didn't look at Jesse as he spoke. "Go away, whoever you are. You are nothing to me. Come back in ten years' time as an acrobat or as a wrestler, and perhaps I'll have you."

Jesse turned and left the little inn, the jeers of Nabal and the other drinkers so loud in his ears that they made his head ache all the more. He stumbled eastward down the hot sunlit street of Emmaus and back onto the road that led to Jerusalem, not knowing now where he would go or what he would do. He knew only one thing for a certainty. He could never return to Arad.

At dusk of that same day Jesse stopped beside a little roadside brook, one that had not yet dried up in summer. He took off his sandals, which he had finally put on to make a good impression on Nabal and had forgotten to remove when he left Emmaus, and looked ruefully at them. They were little more than shredded leather by now. He would have to find work in Jerusalem at once, he told himself. He had almost no money left, and his sandals must be replaced. But what kind of work could he do? He'd been a shepherd most of his life, but who needed shepherds in the city? That was a silly thought. But perhaps in a carpenter's shop Jesse could be useful? He had helped his father and uncle sometimes, and he knew how to hold a board steady and how to use a plane and adze to make wood smooth.

Sunk deeply in thought, Jesse didn't see the tall curly-haired boy who came quietly down the hill behind him to flop on his stomach in one swift movement, put his face in the water and drink. He heard him, though. He heard his shout as he sprang to his feet.

"Hey, who are you? My name is Saul."

Jesse went through the usual hateful gestures to show that he could hear but not speak. He gazed at the other boy in open curiosity. Saul seemed friendly.

Saul's hair was a burnished brown, his brown-and-blue robe even more tattered than Jesse's. His face was broad where Jesse's was thin, and his nose was a snub above a wide mouth. His teeth flashed in a smile as he came out onto the road.

"So you don't talk, huh? Can you tell me what your name is, though, and where you're going?" he said as he sank down beside the other boy. Then he added the common greeting of Israel; "Peace be with you."

Jesse pointed eastward toward Jerusalem and scratched his name in the thick dust. It was easy to write here, far easier than in Jerusalem, where he'd had to use his fingernails in the hard-packed dirt beside the Gate of Ephraim.

"Oh, 'Jesse'! That's your name? I can read some —a little—more than I want to. I don't need to know how to read. It was pretty hard teaching me," Saul commented, then went on. "So you're going to Jerusalem? Well, I'm not! I'm headed the other way. I'm going to the sea to find a ship. Then I'll get on it and go to Rome. I'm going to be rich. A man in Jerusalem told me that they always need people like me in Rome—people who can do what I can do."

Saul looked expectantly and hopefully at Jesse out of yellow-brown eyes. "Do you want to see what I can do?"

Jesse jerked his head to show he meant "yes."

But Saul looked over his shoulder first. "I ran away from my stepfather's house," he told the other boy. "He wanted to make a potter out of me, but I wasn't going to sit beside a potter's wheel all day for the rest of my life the way he does—not when I can do what other boys in Hebron can't do. I used to live in Hebron. I don't know if my stepfather'll come after me or not. If he catches me, he'll beat me. I have to be careful."

Now Saul rose, tucked his robe up, and while Jesse watched open-mouthed did seven cartwheels and four backflips and then came back to Jesse walking on his hands.

"It saves sandal leather. I saw a performer, a Greek, do this once in Jerusalem, and when I went back to Hebron, I started to practice. I've been practicing for a long time now," he told Jesse, laughing as he flipped back to his feet and picked up one of Jesse's worn sandals. "Are you a runaway, too?" he asked.

Jesse shook his head.

"I can juggle. The Greek did that, too," Saul said in a friendly fashion. "I could teach you how to do that. I know I could. Do you want to go to Rome with me?"

Jesse smiled at Saul. He liked this Saul who did not seem to pity him and who laughed so much. No, Jesse would not go to Rome. Jesse was going back to Emmaus right now. Nabal had told him, Jesse, to come back as an acrobat, but that was impossible. The next best thing was to bring an acrobat to Nabal. Perhaps, then, when Nabal hired Saul, he would hire Jesse, too. Nabal had said something about a dancing donkey, and one of the other men had spoken of an old lion. Jesse had a way with animals. Didn't everyone say that?

The mute boy got to his feet now and strapped on his sandals. He wrote "Emmaus" in the dust and pointed to the west.

Saul didn't understand. "But you were going to Jerusalem."

Jesse grinned at him, rubbed out the word "Emmaus" and drew a whole series of animals, some in cages. Then he drew the outline figures of two boys, one standing on his hands, the other juggling three balls in the air, something Jesse had once seen in Arad when he was a little boy. Performers seldom came to Arad—Greek performers who could walk on their hands, never!

Saul understood this easily enough. "You know where I can find a circus—*now*?" He was overjoyed.

Jesse pointed once more toward Emmaus.

"I'll go there, then," Saul told the other boy. "I can make enough silver working for your circus—if I'm lucky, as I usually am, and no one tries to cheat me, and he'd better not—to pay my passage on a ship bound for Rome. You come along with me. I'll look out for you."

Saul reached out and took Jesse's pouch from his belt, doing this so quickly that the mute boy was surprised. "You have a shekel and a lepton," he told his new traveling companion, "and you have some cheese left." Saul tossed the purse back to Jesse. Then he gave his own to the other boy, who looked inside it because Saul wanted him to. Saul had four leptons—Israel's smallest Roman coin—a hunk of bread and half a dozen dried figs.

The acrobat-to-be clapped Jesse on the shoulder. "We're as rich as old King David in his great palace in Jerusalem ever was," he said loudly. "One shekel, five leptons and a good supper like this will take us anywhere we want to go. We'll camp right here and make a fire. How lucky I was to fall in with you today. It must be because of my amulet." He showed it to the other boy. "It's a fox's tooth, a real tooth. I wish it was a gallows' nail. They're even more lucky, and I'll keep looking for one. Now you go get us some wood, Jesse. I'm lucky—stick with me."

Jesse began to gather the hard-to-find firewood by the light of the rising full moon. Saul did not see the mute boy's odd twisted smile. Jesse's thoughts were strange ones. He had little real doubt now that Nabal would hire the accomplished Saul. Jesse, himself, had no strong wish to see the harsh-tongued circus owner again, but it seemed he must. What else could he do if he was not to starve?

III. BELSHAZZAR

Jesse knew where to find Nabal—at the inn of Gezer, as they had arrived at midday.

This time Nabal sat alone, glowering while he drank his wine. He looked up at Jesse when the boy pulled at his sleeve and scowled. Then he muttered, "Get away from me, you! I have nothing for you. Leave me alone! I told you once. How many times must I tell you this?"

But this time Jesse would not go. He pointed desperately to Saul as the man batted at him to leave him alone. Then the mute boy made a sweeping gesture as he backed away.

Saul, knowing the agreed-upon signal, took a deep breath and went over onto his hands. He walked about Gezer's tables on them while the innkeeper and others watched. He did a backflip and finally ended by standing on his head scissoring his legs wildly in the air.

"I suppose you can't speak either?" Nabal had been a very careful observer of Saul's performance.

"Of course I can," Saul answered him, so loudly that the whitewashed walls of the inn rang with the sound of his voice.

"What else can you do, boy?"

The acrobat shrugged. "Many things—many more tricks than I've had space to show you here in this cramped inn. I can juggle, too." He reached for two pomegranates on one of the tables.

Nabal shook his head. "I will watch you do these things later. Go to my circus and ask for Malachi, my helper. Do not perform here—whoever you are and whatever your name is. You're hired. *Never* give a free performance!"

"My name is Saul and I know already about giving things away. It's a stupid thing to do," came from the boy. "I know that I am the best acrobat in Judea, if not in the whole world, and I know that you need an acrobat. But if I join your circus, my friend here joins too." Saul pointed to Jesse.

"And what is *he* to do?"

"He has a way with animals. He'll look after your beasts." After desperately drawing dozens of them in the dust, Jesse had finally made the other boy realize that he liked animals.

Nabal laughed sharply. So did Gezer, who had come to sit down with the circus owner. "Just how did a mute tell you all this?" asked the innkeeper.

Saul grinned at Nabal. "Oh, Jesse has his ways. He can tell me anything he wants to tell me."

Jesse didn't smile. He only nodded at Saul's easy comment, but he wanted to sigh when he thought of the long hours he had spent beside the road the night before as he drew pictures, made gestures and acted out dramas to get Saul to understand the things he wanted to tell him. And the hours that lay ahead of him trying to communicate with Saul and with strangers made him tremble.

Jesse had not actually wanted to become a scribe in Arad, but now that he had left the village of his childhood, he did. If he could write well, he'd have no need of words, he decided. It was a new and foolish dream, but the mute boy cherished it. Dreams cost nothing.

As they left the inn of Gezer, following Nabal's instructions where to find his circus, Jesse looked out of the corner of his eye at Saul, who was strong, confident and happy. Saul caught his glance and smiled at him. "Nabal doesn't seem so bad to me. My stepfather, the potter, was worse. We'll get along fine in his circus until we get some money ahead. Then we'll both go to Rome."

Saul flung his arm around Jesse's shoulder as the two boys went through Emmaus.

The circus of Nabal was a shabby one. Even to Saul's uneducated eye it looked seedy, and he told the other boy so. Jesse's nose had told him this at once. Nabal's patched and torn tents were pitched in a little meadow not far from the village. The breeze hummed through the holes of the largest as Saul and Jesse went inside, inquiring for Malachi.

Malachi was a thinner man than Nabal but had the same thick features and swarthy coloring. Jesse learned later that the two men were half brothers, but it was Nabal who ruled the circus.

Malachi was counting some small coins but scooped them up suspiciously and put them into a bag when the two boys came into the tent. "Who are you? What do you want?" he demanded. His voice was a rasp.

"Peace be with you. Nabal hired me. I'm the new acrobat," Saul told him.

"I was an acrobat once myself," came from Malachi sourly, as if he resented the fact that Saul was younger and stronger.

"Do you want to see what I can do, too?" Saul asked him.

Malachi waved his hand. "No, I don't. If Nabal hired you, that's his affair. That creature behind you—who's he?" He pointed to Jesse, who eyed him with suspicion and dislike.

"Jesse. He's your new animal trainer."

Malachi rumbled. It might have been a laugh. "He doesn't look to me as if he could tend to a crow or sparrow, let alone to camels. Can you cure a sick beast, boy?"

Jesse didn't know what to do now, but Saul's quick answer saved him. "Jesse's a mute. He doesn't talk. But I know that he can cure sick animals!" Saul lied smoothly.

Now Malachi grunted. "Well, it's nothing to me that he doesn't speak if he can handle animals. There's too much talk around here anyhow. Who cares whether he talks or not? The animals certainly won't. Go find the beasts. You won't need to ask where they are. Your noses will tell you soon enough."

Following an unpleasant odor, the boys started to walk by five men who were squatting around a campfire eating. Two of them were huge men in short garments and heavy sandals laced high on their thick legs. A third had an eye patch, and the other two were tall reddish-haired light-eyed men.

"Galileans," Saul whispered to Jesse, who had never before seen a fair-haired man from the northern province of Israel.

One of the tall men from Galilee threw Saul a large hunk of wheat bread, fine bread eaten only by the rich. The boy caught it deftly. "Thank you, may heaven be with you," Saul called out to him.

The one-eyed man spoke to the boys. "Give no

thanks for that. We saw you come out of Malachi's tent just now. Eat while there's something to eat around here. That's what we do. Reuben, here—" he jerked his thumb toward the biggest man—"Reuben, the wrestler, stole the bread for us."

"You'd think I'd be too big not to be caught, wouldn't you?" Reuben was pleased with himself and said so in a high soft voice.

The one-eyed man called out to Jesse, "Hey, you —the skinny one. You're just the sort we need to get us a couple of ducks and fat geese. I know where there's a courtyard full of 'em in Emmaus. You have to creep under a low wall to get at 'em, and none of the rest of us can do that. Have a care of vipers, though."

Jesse shrank back. He'd never stolen anything and he had a terror of horned vipers.

The clever one-eyed man spotted his movement of alarm and disgust. "Never stole before, huh? I see that clear enough. Well, ye'll learn to steal fast here to keep your stomach from cavin' in to meet yer backbone."

Reuben grunted in agreement, then said, "What my friend here tells you is true enough. Nabal feeds his animals enough to keep 'em alive, but he don't feed us hardly at all. And it takes a lot of food to keep me and my wrestling partner ready to crack each other's ribs for people to pay to see us."

Saul laughed very easily, Jesse thought. He could

even laugh at Reuben's and the one-eyed man's ominous words. Jesse wondered if Saul had ever stolen. Perhaps he had, but, if so, it didn't seem to have hurt Saul much. Still and all, thieving was against the Law—the laws of Moses the rabbi in Arad had carefully taught him.

The boys followed their noses as Malachi had told them and came to where the animals were tethered.

Nabal owned two camels, three mules, seven donkeys and one lion, which was confined in a cage with rusty bars. The boys looked at the lion first. Flies crawled over his twitching skin. A half-eaten bone lay under one paw as Nabal's old lion slept, snoring. The floor of his cage was filthy.

"That's what smells the worst, I think." Saul was wrinkling up his nose. "I'll ask Reuben about cleaning out the cage."

Jesse agreed with his friend. Something should be done for the old lion. Neither boy could eat the bread the Galilean had thrown them now.

While Saul remained staring at the sleeping lion, Jesse went to look at the camels. They weren't in bad shape—even if they were far too thin. They were tall yellowish beasts who stared down at Jesse ben Abdiel in the superior manner of camels. Although camels weren't commonly seen in Israel, Jesse knew all too well that all camels hated all people. The boy sighed deeply. He didn't much like camels. He hoped he wouldn't have to tend them.

The mules were next, tethered on a line. They weren't well kept and badly needed currying and brushing. The leather water buckets near them were empty, but there was a little stone-filled brook nearby. Jesse picked up a bucket, a bone-dry bucket. The animals had not been watered all day.

Saul joined his friend while they examined the donkeys, also tethered on a line. Six were brownish and ordinary-looking, big donkeys from Lycaonia but slat-thin.

But the seventh was different—very different. A Muscat ass, he was smaller than the others, so light a gray he was almost white. He was tied separately to a sycamore tree a good distance away from the other donkeys. He wore an old red leather harness with tassels, most of them missing, on the breast strap, but on his halter between his eyes someone had tied a red rag as a talisman to keep him from falling down.

As the boys approached this donkey, he lifted his drooping head and bared his long yellow teeth. The gleam in his eye was an evil one. As Jesse and Saul passed behind him, carefully skirting his hindquarters, the seventh donkey lunged backward at his rope, striking out with his hooves. He missed kicking the boys and brayed his disappointment to the sky so thunderously that Jesse put his hands over his ears.

"That one has a bad temper," exclaimed Saul after the whitish donkey had finished braying. The two boys had retreated in a hurry to where the camels stood. The large animals moved about restlessly because of the donkey's din.

Jesse touched one of the buckets with his foot and jerked his head. Saul nodded. Although he was a potter by trade, he knew something about beasts, and Jesse was grateful for this. It would make his work easier. "All right, I see what you mean, Jesse. We'll water the animals first, and then we'll clean out the lion's cage."

So back and forth to the brook the two boys went, bringing fresh water to Nabal's hungry, thirsty animals. They kept a good distance from the seventh donkey, though, because they very soon learned that they couldn't get a bucket to him without danger from his teeth or his hooves.

The one-eyed man showed up as they lugged the second bucketful to the camels. "Hmm. It's not so wise to start out working hard, lads," he told them. He meant to be kind, Jesse guessed, but he still didn't like the man. "What if Nabal and Malachi get wind of what you're doin'? It'll give 'em ideas about how the rest of us ought to work. Don't do any more than you got to do. Nabal, he don't pay us half of the time, and we steal our own food. Why should we work hard for him?"

Saul grinned at him, then said, "They were thirsty

and hungry and so are we. Got any more of that good bread?"

"No," said the one-eyed man. "Maybe Nabal'll bring somethin' from Emmaus. When he wins at dice, sometimes he does. There are six more of us—two boxers, the ropedancer and the other bareback rider besides me. Yes, I do that and handle the old lion, too. The others are out in Emmaus and in the countryside now, lookin' for somethin' to bring back with 'em. Malachi wouldn't let the knife thrower go today—he's sick. And the fortuneteller, he's much too grand to go out lookin' around for things." Now the man stared hard at Jesse out of his one little eye. "You take a look at old Belshazzar yet?"

"The donkey tethered down at the end, away from the others?" Saul answered for his friend. "That's the donkey in the red harness?"

"That's the one I mean, acrobat. That one's Belshazzar, the dancin' donkey."

"Oh," came from Saul. "He tried to kick us."

Jesse listened, an empty bucket still in his hand, as the lion handler spoke. The man was smiling, but it was a joyless smile. "He's done worse'n that. He's the meanest animal in Israel. He was mean when Nabal bought him ten years back, and he's got meaner every year since then. We used to think he'd get better when he got older 'n' weaker, but not him. I'll show you how to handle him." He picked up a stick that lay on the ground and walked boldly up to the seventh donkey, who laid back his ears and showed his teeth.

Crack! Crack! went the stick on Belshazzar's back, and the donkey leaped and lashed out at his tormentor with his feet, but the one-eyed man skillfully jumped aside.

"Here you, the skinny one who don't have anything to say, come on now and look at him! I'll show you how old Belshazzar works. The only thing he understands is this stick. The bigger the stick the better he dances!"

Now the man beat the donkey twice on his left flank, and the animal rose up into the air prancing. When he was struck once on the right flank he lifted one front hoof and then the other in a stiff jerky little dance step. "You got to find out all the tricks this old donkey knows for yerself. He's got a whole lot of tricks—dirty ones, mostly. Trainers won't put up with him long. He's had a hundred handlers. I wonder how long *you'll* last? What's your name?" He was looking at Jesse now.

"He's Jesse," Saul replied. "I'm Saul."

"Well, Jesse and Saul, I told you about Belshazzar, didn't I?"

Jesse stood close enough now to the white donkey to see his scars, dozens of them. The boy thought he could identify the scars made by camel and horse teeth and the places where Belshazzar's skin had been broken by blows from his handlers.

Saul, who'd courageously brought the seventh donkey water, saw them too. He caught Jesse's eye on him and seemed to understand what the mute boy felt. "Don't beat this one any more, now," Saul told the one-eyed man, who lounged with his back against the tree. "Jesse and I don't want to see him dance again. That's what Nabal told us—'Never give a free performance.' Anyway, I want to clean up your old lion's cage if I can."

The lion handler chuckled at this. "You can just open the door and roust him out if you want to. Old King Solomon hasn't been able to bite anybody for the last five years. He just worries his bones now. He hasn't got the strength to spring on a man. It scares the wits out of him to leave his cage, where he's safe. But I'll go get Reuben and have him hold Solomon while you slosh out the cage. Reuben'll be able to keep him from jumping back in till yer done—not that it'd matter. Solomon, he'd just snore while you cleaned things up inside the cage with him, boy."

Saul laughed. While they waited for Reuben, he and Jesse sat on a rock and watched the seventh donkey gulp water from the bucket. It seemed to both boys from the way the white donkey drank that he had not been watered for a long time. The other animals had not been half so thirsty. Because of Belshazzar's temper, Jesse ben Abdiel guessed, no one wanted to come near him.

"Well, we've been hired, Jesse," Saul told his friend from Arad. "It seems to me that we've got plenty to do, too. That old donkey's going to be a lot of hard work, isn't he?"

Jesse nodded and picked up the stick the one-eyed man had used. He'd had an idea while he watched the donkey dance. It was an idea worth trying, and if it worked he could throw away the stick forever. A trick he'd taught the dog, Tob, had given him the idea. If Belshazzar was clever enough to be a dancing donkey, Belshazzar could be clever enough to learn a new way of doing things. Jesse only hoped that the animal was not too old—it was more difficult to teach things to old animals. Belshazzar *was* old, though, and even if they had long lives, donkeys didn't live forever. Would it be worth all the work he had in mind, Jesse ben Abdiel asked himself?

IV. THE DECREE
FROM CAESAR AUGUSTUS

A week after Jesse and Saul joined the circus, Nabal
decided it was time to leave Emmaus. The innkeeper, Gezer, who readily took Nabal's money for
wine, didn't care if the circus stayed, but the farmers
who missed geese and ducks and the village shop-
keepers who had lost loaves of bread and sweet grain
cakes to the quick fingers of bareback riders, boxers
and the agile young ropedancer were up in arms.

So Nabal's people took down their tents, packed

50

them onto the backs of the donkeys and left Emmaus, traveling to the east.

By now Jesse ben Abdiel had learned several things. One night as they sat beside the little campfire the performers had made, Reuben the wrestler and the one-eyed man told the boys why Nabal's circus did not return to Jerusalem.

Reuben threw a duck bone over his shoulder and wiped his hands on his bare knees. "If you asked me right now," he said loudly, "I'd go back to Jerusalem tomorrow and take my chances with the Romans."

"Not I," said the one-eyed man with a hard laugh. "I'll not put my hide in danger again. Not one of us can show his face in Jerusalem again, except for these two brats here—" he gestured with an empty wine cup toward Saul and Jesse—"and that's only because nobody there has ever set eyes on them before, that I know of. The rest of us would be picked up and crucified as thieves by the Romans, right away. It was a narrow thing back there, Reuben, when the old juggler got caught stealing those pigeons for the pot. They crucified him fast enough —and you know how we were warned."

"Yes," added one of the fair Galileans. "We were told to take ourselves out of Jerusalem and to stay out of it."

Reuben sighed. "They even escorted us to the city gates. But all the same I miss Jerusalem. I miss the beautiful women whose sandals with each step send up a mist of perfume. I miss their soft bright eyes above their veils upon me, admiring me as I wrestle. These red-faced country wenches do not interest me. I would go back to Jerusalem if I could."

"Ah, but Reuben, you can't!" put in the one-eyed man, cutting off further talk about the beautiful women of Jerusalem. "We must avoid Jerusalem as we avoid lepers. From now on, thanks to that old fool juggler's fondness for pigeon and his clumsiness, we go only to country towns. If you ask me, Roman crucifixion was too good for him." He turned, grinning at the boys. "You two are young and swift. You'll take easily to being taught the trade that keeps us alive because Nabal either can't or won't."

Jesse stared at him in alarm. No, Nabal's lion handler was not playing a game with them. He meant they were to steal. His grin was that of a wolf. Now the mute boy looked in alarm at Saul. The would-be great acrobat's eyes were on his crossed feet, and his face was sober. But Saul did not protest as Jesse ben Abdiel had hoped he would.

"I see by your faces that you don't fancy the work, and maybe the cross if you get caught at it, eh?" commented Reuben. "It's the same risk all of us run, though, and why should we run it alone to feed the likes of you two? When your belly's empty enough, you'll thieve. We won't feed you much longer on what we get. It's time you did your share."

Two days after that Saul stole for the first time—
a fat hen from a farmer's courtyard. His tutor was
the ropedancer, a young man from Ashkelon, a city
on the seacoast. Unlike the other performers the
ropedancer was not a Jew but a Philistine, so the
laws of Moses did not bother him. He had never
heard "Thou shalt not steal." He taught Saul how
to worm his way on his stomach silently into any
place he chose to go. Before long Saul was a good
thief. In the village of Ephraim the ropedancer told
Saul there was nothing more he could teach him,
and to Jesse's disgust the acrobat even seemed
pleased to hear the praise.

For a week or so Saul shared what he stole with
Jesse, because the others no longer gave the mute
boy anything. But then one day he said, "See here,
Jesse ben Abdiel, I know the Law, too. I don't like
to steal. I have to. But I'm not going to steal to feed
you any more than Reuben and the others will steal
to keep you and me from starving. I don't blame
them either, and you shouldn't blame me. I'm not
going to spend the shekels I've saved for food.
They're going to be my passage money to Rome.
You're going to have to steal for yourself, Jesse!"

And with these words and without a backward
glance Saul walked off to help one of the Galileans,
who called to him to help set up Nabal's tent. Jesse
looked after his friend mournfully. Saul had changed
in the little time Jesse had known him. He was

harder. Jesse believed it was the life in the circus
—not Saul himself. He found it impossible to hate
Saul the way he hated Nabal and the others. The
mute boy sighed. Yes, he would have to steal, too,
but not until he was faint with hunger.

In Tekoa, another country town, Jesse gave in and
took a carp from a fish pond, a fine carp that made
the ropedancer praise his skill. "You have the mak-
ings of a good thief, lad," said the Philistine in his
poor Aramaic. "I prophesy you'll be a better one
than your acrobat friend."

And so Jesse was. In Beth-zur he stole a duck
and a cock, but it cost him a very painful scorpion
sting as he crawled under a thorn hedge. "Better a
scorpion than an asp," Reuben told the boy. "Watch
out carefully for snakes from now on."

By the time Nabal had taken his circus to the
Jordan Valley in the month of Tishri, Jesse was an
expert thief. He could wriggle into places where
Saul's expanding shoulders would not permit him
to go.

Jesse needed his strength. Traveling was hard
work, and Jesse, unlike Nabal and Malachi, never
rode a mule. He walked. By choice, he walked
beside Belshazzar wherever Nabal took them on the
road. The surly donkey attracted him more and
more. For weeks the mute boy had tried to gain the
white donkey's confidence. Jesse ben Abdiel was
the only one to groom and curry him. He tended

to the open wounds on the animal's back. He pulled grass for Belshazzar and brought him his water and hay. He constantly dodged hooves and drew back from Belshazzar's long teeth. How he wished he could speak soothingly to the donkey. But Jesse could only look at the animal with mournful eyes and be very gentle when he touched him. He was sorry for the mistreated beast.

Finally, in Tekoa, the same day he had stolen the carp, Belshazzar let him move near him without skinning back his teeth.

Soon Jesse began to handle the donkey himself. This happened in the Jordan Valley, the fruit-filled vale where no one noticed or cared when a hungry boy took figs from a fig tree. There were hundreds of orchards and so few men to tend them. At that, it was hardly stealing. In Israel beggars had a right to take what they needed from field and orchard as long as they did not carry a basket or a sickle. In the Jordan Valley, Jesse felt safe and his stomach was full. Sometimes he almost felt like playing his shepherd's pipes. For some reason that he did not understand he did not want the circus folk to hear his music, but the beautiful Jordan Valley made the boy happy. He liked its lush hot greenness, so different from Judea's brown dry hills.

So did Belshazzar. In northern Judea the white donkey had ailed. His legs had grown more and more stiff, it seemed to Jesse, as the one-eyed man put him through his paces with his stick. But in the hot moist air of the Jordan Valley the donkey danced better. And Belshazzar's temper had seemed to mellow toward everyone—not only the mute boy. Jesse didn't have so much trouble now keeping him from fighting with the other circus animals.

Once when no one was watching, Jesse untied the donkey, who followed him obediently to the side of the flowing Jordan. Jesse meant to try out the idea he'd had months before in Emmaus. This was his first real chance. He took up a small stick, one that would not hurt the donkey at all, and with it he put Belshazzar through his whole set of tricks.

Delighted with his success, the boy ran back to the camp pulling at the donkey's halter as Belshazzar trotted behind. He caught Saul's attention by toppling the acrobat over as the other boy was doing a practice headstand. "What's the matter with you, Jesse?" Saul yelled angrily at his friend.

Jesse made wild gestures, prancing a little himself, as if he were the dancing donkey, and held out the little switch he'd brought with him from the river. Then, as Saul watched, lying flat on the ground eating a stolen apricot, Jesse put Belshazzar through his paces with only the switch. Other performers and Malachi came to watch.

Reuben called out in approval as the donkey made his usual final bow. "Who would have thought it?"

"Not I," said the Philistine ropedancer.

"That's how the animal will dance from now on," grunted Malachi. "The mute here will handle him —not anyone else. The beast's old. Beating him with a stick will only kill him off faster. This way's better." Without a word of thanks Malachi went off to his tent.

But Jesse, who had not expected praise, stood beaming when Malachi had gone. He felt like hugging the white donkey, but he didn't dare. He didn't really have that much confidence in Belshazzar's temper yet. The donkey might bite off his nose.

At the end of the month of Tishri, Nabal decided it was time they left the Jordan Valley. They had performed wherever they could, but the tax collectors, men who wore brass plates on their chests and carried stout sticks, were showing more than a passing interest in him and his circus. Nabal had learned this in a tavern. He did not intend to be caught and forced to pay a single lepton to any tax collector. Taxes were very heavy in Israel. Rome demanded much tribute, and so did the temple in Jerusalem. Nabal intended to support neither—not unless he was forced to it.

So they left, traveling westward toward the colder seacoast once more. This made Jesse ben Abdiel sad. He hated to leave the place where he'd had so much success with Belshazzar and where the little donkey had seemed so well. What would happen to Belshazzar in Judea now? What would happen to him, too, Jesse asked himself. Nabal had chosen the town of Arimathea. Would the dancing donkey perform so well for Jesse there?

Jesse watched the white donkey carefully as they traveled again past Jerusalem to the west. Belshazzar stumbled often now in the deep cart ruts, and his head was lower than when they'd left northern Judea for the Jordan Valley. He was failing fast. Concerned, Jesse stole grain from Nabal's own riding mule to give to Belshazzar. With each Roman milestone they passed along the road to Arimathea, the boy became more worried about the donkey— the animal he'd come to think of as his own in spite of his warnings to himself that Belshazzar belonged to Nabal.

When they reached Arimathea, the boy threw away the switch he had used, afraid that even it was too much for the donkey's flagging strength. Belshazzar had learned how to dance—although he seemed more stiff than ever—with only nudges from Jesse's hand.

Saul was so surprised when Jesse showed him what new things the donkey could do that he ran to fetch both Nabal and Malachi from the tavern. Both men watched carefully as the donkey performed for them. Jesse had hoped this time to hear words of praise for his hard work with the animal —but no, he did not receive them.

Malachi spoke first to his half brother. "Belshaz-

zar's slower than he was before we went to the
Jordan Valley, Nabal. He doesn't lift up his hooves
as high as he did."

"I can see that," snapped Nabal, his eyes on the
little donkey as he painfully performed his dance.
"I've got eyes in my head, haven't I? We've got to
get us another smart donkey soon, very soon. And
perhaps the mute here—" he gestured toward Jesse
—"can teach him to dance too. After all, somebody
taught this animal, didn't he—a hundred years ago?"
Nabal laughed harshly at his jest.

"What will we do with this one?" asked Malachi.

"Get rid of him! If King Solomon had enough
teeth left to chew, I'd know a very good place for
Belshazzar to end up." Nabal laughed again, not
seeing how Jesse had gone white with shock and
horror.

"He's too stringy even for the young lions of
Caesar Augustus in Rome," said Malachi. "Perhaps
some fool will take him off our hands. Perhaps someone will buy him—someone who's blind, maybe?"

Nabal clapped his half brother on the shoulder.
"Well, then, Malachi, you keep close watch for a
fool. Any fool who will buy old Belshazzar must be
the biggest fool in all Israel."

As the two men went to their tent, Jesse did a
desperate thing—something he'd not dared before.
He flung his arms around Belshazzar's neck and
rested his face against the donkey's. Belshazzar did

not try to bite him. The donkey stood motionless. Jesse found himself wanting to speak to Belshazzar more badly than he had ever wanted to speak to anyone else—even his father, Abdiel. He wanted to cry out, "Wherever you'll be going, I'll go, too! I won't stay here to train another donkey. No, I won't! I'll go with you!"

Then the boy truly admitted to himself what he'd known ever since he'd first made Belshazzar dance for him back in the Jordan Valley. He loved the white donkey—more than he had loved Tob in Arad, far more than he loved Saul. Jesse needed this one special animal to love. His thoughts were very bitter ones. He remembered what Nabal had laughingly said about him and Belshazzar some days before. "One dumb animal gets on well with another. They deserve each other."

Nabal's words had been right after all. Once more Jesse cried out in his mind to the donkey, "I guess that's why I love you, Belshazzar. You and I are alike. Neither of us can talk and nobody really wants either one of us."

There were quite a few little villages around Arimathea, and Nabal found it profitable to take his little circus to them, so they spent several months in northwestern Judea. The nights grew more and more cold. Jesse gave up one of the coverlets he had stolen and put it over Belshazzar. The boy, who now shivered himself each night, thought the coverlet helped the donkey somewhat. His worries grew ever worse. Belshazzar found it more difficult each morning to get up on his rapidly stiffening legs, and now he needed help—Jesse pulling on one side of him while Saul pushed on the other. And the donkey grew weaker day by day. The chill dry winds blowing from the desert by day and the cold by night sapped his strength.

One afternoon Saul, who had gone into Arimathea with Nabal, came bounding up to Jesse, who sat, his robe pulled close about him, beside a shivering Belshazzar. The donkey was too listless even to nibble at the drying grass. "Peace be with you, Jesse, we're leaving Arimathea in the morning," Saul told his friend excitedly. Jesse looked at Saul with a question in his eyes—not a very interested question.

"We're going to Bethlehem," said Saul.

Jesse shrugged, his face a sour study. He had seen Bethlehem. He'd seen Tekoa and Ephraim and Emmaus. What was so special about Bethlehem— just another village in Judea? Now if it had been the warm Jordan Valley they were to return to, that would be different.

Saul dropped to his knees beside Jesse. "There was a herald at the inn in Arimathea. He spoke our tongue, but he really came from Caesar Augustus. He read us a decree from Rome." Saul laughed. "What he said made Nabal angry! He got so angry that after the herald left, he smashed an inn table

with his fists and feet. The herald said that all Jews
have to go back to the place where their house came
from to be counted and to pay the tribute that
Caesar Augustus demands. Nabal and Malachi are
of the house of David, so they have to go to Bethlehem. You know how Nabal hates to pay taxes or
tribute."

Jesse nodded. He didn't care about Caesar Augustus, hundreds of miles away across the sea in
Rome. It didn't matter to him if Nabal had to pay
tribute or not. If he knew Nabal, the man would find
some way to cheat the tax gatherers. It was Belshazzar who worried him.

Bethlehem was far away from Arimathea.

Saul guessed what Jesse was thinking. He sometimes still did, although the times were ever rarer.
Now he got up and examined the white donkey
carefully, then lifted each little hoof in turn. Belshazzar had become either so gentle or so weary
that he permitted others near him now.

"He'll be fine, Jesse," Saul said, lying. "He'll dance
for the house of David in Bethlehem. There'll be
hundreds of people going there. That's what Nabal
says. He says that's the only good thing about our
going there." Saul paused for a moment. "I'm from
the house of David too, come to think of it. But no
Roman's going to squeeze even one lepton out of
me—not my passage money to Rome. I'll dodge them
all right. What about you, Jesse?"

The mute boy paid no heed to Saul's question. He was not of the house of David, but what did it matter when Belshazzar was so ill? He didn't care about the Romans and their emperor's decree. He sat staring unhappily at the grass at his feet as Saul walked away to tell the news that they left for Bethlehem to Reuben and the ropedancer.

They left Arimathea that next morning and started on their way. Already the people of Israel were abroad on their journeys to the homes of their ancestors to be taxed by Rome. Whole families left Arimathea as Nabal's circus did. By midday the road that led east was clogged with oxcarts and donkeys. A new stream of people came from each little village along the way. Because the Israelites obeyed the decree of Caesar Augustus, no matter how unwillingly, Nabal's pace was a slow one along the roads. This slow pace pleased Jesse. It pleased him even more in the days ahead, when the circus and everyone else moved to the side of the road to permit the Roman couriers to sweep by on swift horses on their way to the seaports, Ashkelon, Caesarea, Apollonia and Joppa. Anything that made Nabal slow to a complete halt pleased the boy, because it gave Belshazzar more chance to rest. A kinder, more sympathetic Saul helped his friend now. All of Nabal's donkeys carried packs, but each morning Saul, more clever with his hands than Jesse ben Abdiel, put a pack on Belshazzar with nothing in it but one of Nabal's softest sleeping mats and much air, plumping the mat up well until the white donkey's burden looked as heavy as any of the others.

Neither Nabal nor Malachi ever seemed to notice Saul's trick, although both men went by often, cursing when they had to move out into a field to give room to someone more important or to lag behind a particularly slow oxcart carrying a family to eastern Judea.

Belshazzar moved like a donkey carved of wood. There was no longer any spring at all in his old legs. How, then, could he dance in Bethlehem and make money for Nabal, Jesse fearfully asked himself. The donkey's head sagged almost to the ground as he shuffled, and although he was often thirsty, he ate far less grain and grass than before. Jesse was deeply worried and slept badly—almost as badly as Belshazzar, who groaned in his light sleep.

And as they turned south toward Bethlehem, Jesse slept even more badly. So did everyone who was on the road to that little city.

It was because of the star—the great white star! No one knew its name. It had come blazing out of the heavens, a sudden explosion of light to illumine the night sky, making it bright as day. Wherever Nabal's circus went by day, the white star found it by night. The only way a person could sleep was inside his tent with a coverlet or cloak pulled over his head. Nabal and Malachi cursed the star that made their half-starved animals more restless than a full moon did. They cursed King Solomon, whose roars woke them up when they'd finally been able to fall asleep. The wrestlers and the one-eyed man were uneasy about the strange star, and so were Saul and Jesse. The one-eyed man asked the fat fortuneteller about it in Jesse's hearing one evening as the little circus camped for the night.

"I know the names of the planets, the Egyptian names and the Chaldean names," said the fortuneteller, "but I have never seen or heard of anything like this before." Saul, sitting beside Jesse, chuckled softly to hear the conceited man finally admit there was something he did not know. The fortuneteller went on, "Now it is possible that several of the great planets have met together in the heavens or have collided. Yes, that is possible." He tilted his head to look up at the star and then looked quickly away again because of its great brilliance.

"But what does it mean?" Saul had very little patience with Nabal's chief favorite, the fortuneteller, who was a great liar and cheat and who sent Saul out before him to enter each village to ask questions and to eavesdrop to find out what men there had money, what their names were, the number of sheep and goats they owned, the number of marriageable daughters—anything that would help him amaze country fools by the wise replies he could give them to the questions they might ask him. The rabbis of Israel hated astrologers and fortunetellers, calling them wicked men, but the common folk flocked to them to learn the future and paid high prices to hear what they wanted to hear. Nabal's fortuneteller always obliged the people who came to him.

"If it is truly a conjunction of planets or if it is a newborn star, it means but one thing. Something very remarkable is about to happen!" the astrologer replied. This time he was sure of his information, Jesse knew.

"Something good or something bad?" Reuben asked respectfully.

The fortuneteller chuckled. "Who knows that? Something bad, very possibly. Perhaps King Herod is going to die?" He winked at this. "But it could be something else even more evil. I do not personally believe that Nabal will be able to avoid paying the tax gatherers in Bethlehem. That would be a bad thing for Nabal, wouldn't it?" And with these words, the man started into his tent, but he turned at the entrance and said, "As for the rest of you, you rabble Nabal calls a circus, you come from all over creation. You'll scatter like chaff in the wind when the tax collectors come near. I doubt if you, Reuben, and the other wrestler have ever had homes or parents. How could a Roman collect from you? As for me,

I don't intend to pay one lepton to any Roman. I don't intend to pay anything at all, and I'll shower my most potent curses on the Roman that asks me. That will chill his bones—even Roman bones. But then I don't own this wretched circus either—a thing for which I am eternally grateful."

The next day they turned onto the crowded way to Bethlehem—onto the road that led south from Jerusalem. The way was even more clogged, now that the people from the north as well as the west had come onto it—people from Jerusalem, Jericho, Bethany, people from all of northern Israel. But Jesse saw only Belshazzar, who stumbled with every other step. The boy motioned to Saul and made the other boy understand that they should walk on either side of the white donkey to keep him hidden from the sharp eyes of Malachi and Nabal. Jesse had put the red harness on him that morning. Often during the day he and Saul grabbed the harness and pulled on it to help Belshazzar over a rut in the road or to keep his feet when some other animal jostled him.

Saul now told Jesse the truth the mute boy knew all too well in his heart. "Belshazzar's very sick, Jesse. We'd better watch out for Nabal. Malachi won't be any problem. He just rode on ahead to Bethlehem to find an inn for us. But Nabal's been sniffing around the donkey already today. I saw him. It was while you were still asleep this morning.

Nabal was out of his tent early. The star wouldn't let him sleep."

Jesse nodded miserably. He had overslept that morning. Once during the night he'd thought he'd heard Belshazzar bray, and he'd got up and gone outside. What he had seen surprised him. Belshazzar, who usually lay like a log, a moaning log, all night, was on his feet, his head lifted, his eyes fixed on the pure-white star. When Jesse went to him to touch him, the donkey had not even noticed his friend. Sometimes Belshazzar would turn his head to rub it on Jesse's arm, but not this time—no matter what the boy did. The donkey's whole attention was given to the star. Watching Belshazzar until he had lain down again had kept Jesse up too long. That was why he had overslept. The boy sighed. How could anyone be jealous of a star? But Jesse was, because the donkey had ignored him to gaze at it.

Lost in his unhappy thoughts, the mute boy did not once look up as they passed the couple at the side of the road. The woman sat on a large stone while the man stood, leaning on a staff. They were ordinary-looking people, simply dressed, and there were so many ordinary folk abroad in Israel these days—all headed for the traditional home of their ancestors.

But Jesse did look up—in alarm—when Nabal on his mule came hurrying up to his circus, trotting from behind. Nabal liked to bring up the rear, not to be associated with his shabby circus. He liked to talk to rich and important men from Jerusalem also on their way to Bethlehem while Reuben and the one-eyed man led the circus. He liked to pretend he, too, was important. Now Nabal was grinning. "Get away from that donkey, boys," he called out to Jesse and Saul. Then he reached down and grabbed the rope around Belshazzar's neck.

Astonished at the speed with which it had happened, the two boys stood open-mouthed looking on while Belshazzar was pulled at a shambling trot away from them, half dragged by the powerful man. At once Jesse started after Nabal, but Saul held him back. "Let the donkey go, Jesse! Belshazzar belongs to Nabal!" he said to his friend.

Jesse wanted to shout, "No, he's *mine!*" but nothing could come out but a howl of anger and misery. The mute boy shook off Saul's arm and darted away, running, his robe flapping about his ankles, following Nabal.

He must not lose Belshazzar! But Jesse was too late.

Two oxcarts and then a caravan of heavily laden mules blocked his way. He could not dive between the wooden wheels of the carts or under the bellies of the mules. By the time he found Nabal, he found him alone, putting some coins into the leather purse at his waist. Jesse looked frantically up and down the road, but in the moving throng he saw no white donkey.

"I sold him," Nabal called out to the boy as if he expected Jesse to think this was a fine thing. "What a stroke of luck for me." Nabal was in a very good mood. He didn't spy out the tears in the boy's eyes as he reined in his mule to walk back toward the circus at Jesse's side. He didn't even look at the mute. Nabal wanted to talk. Even the strange speechless boy, the boy he usually ignored, would do when a man felt talkative. "A carpenter from Nazareth bought the old donkey. We came along in the nick of time for the carpenter. His old donkey died this morning just outside Jerusalem, and he badly needed an animal for his wife to ride to Bethlehem. Do you know what I told that fool of a Galilean?"

Jesse didn't nod his head to show he'd heard the question, but that didn't hinder the circus owner from rambling on. "I said that this white beast of mine was gentle and strong." Nabal roared with laughter. "With luck, great good luck, Belshazzar may carry the carpenter's wife into Bethlehem, but he won't carry anyone any farther than that. When the carpenter pays his tribute, he can buy another donkey in Bethlehem to take him and his wife back to Nazareth if he has enough money left. He gave me *four* staters for old Belshazzar, who's nothing but vulture's bait!" Nabal laughed again, making

people who were riding by turn to stare at him. "I'll
take my circus to Nazareth next. If carpenters are
so free with their money there, what about the rich
merchants? They'll shower me with shekels and
staters."

By now they had caught up with the circus. Saul
came forward to help Jesse, whose eyes were so filled
with tears that he staggered in the dust of the road
as badly as Belshazzar had done. Saul took his friend
by the arm but spoke to Nabal. "You sold the white
donkey?"

"Yes," said Nabal proudly, "and I got a fine price
for him. Did you see the tall carpenter who bought
him, the man beside the road, the man with the
woman?"

Saul nodded soberly. "I saw him, the bearded man
in the brown robe, and I saw the veiled woman
with the blue cloth over her head. They went by a
little while ago. The woman was riding Belshazzar."

"Wait till I tell Malachi of this piece of good fortune. I'll tell him I found the fool we sought before
he did." Nabal kicked his mule into a trot and left
the boys in his dust at the end of the circus as they
walked behind King Solomon's cage. But before he
was out of sight and lost in the throng, he bawled
to Jesse, "You look after the camels now, boy. That
will be your work from now on."

Saul tried to comfort the other boy. "They seemed
to be good people, Jesse—the people who bought

Belshazzar. The man had a kind face. I couldn't see the woman very well because of her mantle and veil."

Jesse would not be comforted. He had always expected little from people and had come to expect less. But he had not expected such horror as this. He wiped his tears away with the back of his hand, leaving a smear of dirt across his face. Anger against Nabal ate at him like a live thing, while his throat burned with a bitter choking rage.

He scarcely listened as Saul went on. "There'll be a great crowd in Bethlehem tonight. It's a good thing for us that we carry our own tents wherever we go. We're lucky that Nabal didn't try to sell the tents too. We'd better keep an eye on ours, shabby as it is. It's more patches than cloth already." He had tried to make a joke, but then he went on even more soothingly. "Malachi will find us an inn courtyard to give our show. If you want me to do it, I'll ask Nabal to buy another clever donkey just as soon as he can find one for you to train. Maybe one of the pack donkeys will do? Why don't you try to find out if one of them can be taught to dance too? You can do it. You're the best person with animals I ever saw."

Jesse glared at Saul in fury. So Saul thought there could ever be another Belshazzar? So Saul thought that Jesse could so easily be bought off by getting another donkey? Sometimes Saul didn't seem to

understand even the simplest things. Jesse made a
fist to hit his friend. His tears were gone now. Then
in a flash of understanding as bright as the white
star itself, Jesse knew what he would do. He let his
fist fall open and he grinned at the astonished acrobat, who had braced himself for his friend's blow,
deciding that if this was what would make Jesse
feel better, he would put up with it.

This was the sort of thing Saul, who had told
himself more than once that he would never truly
comprehend Jesse, did understand. Saul knew that
particular bright smile of Jesse's. It was almost a
signal between the acrobat and the mute boy. It
meant that his friend had made up his mind about
something.

Saul spoke quietly so no one else would hear.
"Whatever it is that you just thought of, if it makes
you feel as pleased as you look right now, Jesse, you
go ahead and do it. And I'll be behind you to help
if I can. I'll even help you throw Nabal into a well,
a deep one, if that's what you want—and the fortuneteller, too, and Malachi right on top of Nabal."

Still smiling, the mute boy shook his head at this
suggestion. No, he didn't think that Saul would
really approve if he told him. Saul took things pretty
much as he found them. He didn't have much
imagination and he never thought beyond today—
except to save money to pay his passage to Rome.
Saul would argue against it if he knew what Jesse

planned to do—to get Belshazzar back no matter how he had to do it!

The two boys walked along now on the last mile to Bethlehem, just another Judean village of white stone houses ringed by hills.

Saul began to whistle, happy now that his friend was happier. Other travelers looked at Saul, smiled and nudged one another as he turned cartwheels beside the road, until the one-eyed man shouted at him to stop giving "free performances."

But Jesse kept his head down as he went, praying that Belshazzar had had the strength to make it to the little city of David with the carpenter's wife riding on his back.

V. THE THREE KINGS

The great white star burst above the horizon as Nabal's circus descended the hill into the city of David.

The one long street was jammed with people, all come to Bethlehem to be taxed, to pay the tribute Rome demanded. Men wandered up and down. looking for a place to rest while their veiled wives and their round-eyed children stood close by their oxcarts and donkeys, waiting, guarding the belongings they'd brought with them on their forced journey. There was not one man among them who did not hate the Romans in his heart, for every Israelite hated to pay the tribute to the conquerors.

These folk who had come to Bethlehem were the people of the house of David, the house of the great king of Israel, the king who had killed Goliath, the giant, and who had ruled in Jerusalem long, long ago. Jesse remembered how often his father had spoken with wonder of the house of David. The long-promised Messiah was to come out of it. Jesse sniffed. His life with Nabal's circus had driven almost all thoughts of religion away except for his morning and evening prayers, and they were only a habit. He didn't go to the synagogues in the towns the circus played. Nabal didn't like the idea of anyone's going, and moreover his performers, as suspected thieves, were never very welcome. The boy looked carefully at the men and women from the house of David. They weren't any different from the people he had seen in any other village or city of Israel. Some were richly dressed, most were poorly dressed, but they were all the same to him, and like everyone else they turned to stare when they saw the circus jog past. Children pointed to the caged lion, who looked calmly at them, too bored to roar in anger, although Saul, whose job it was when they went through a town, pinched King Solomon's tail in his strong fingers.

Jesse noticed how Nabal rode through Bethlehem. He noticed with hatred. The circus owner rode grandly past the Roman soldiers. Jesse glanced at them, guessing rightly that they'd been sent down from Jerusalem to keep order and to aid the tax gatherers. The soldiers did not seem to see Nabal's pitiful circus, and the man's face turned red with anger for a moment. Nabal didn't want to pay his tribute, but he wanted to be noticed just the same. Saul had seen this too, and it warmed Jesse to hear his friend snicker.

They reached the end of the street. Here Nabal halted. The camel bells stilled as the great animals fell to their knees with sounds of relief—shuddering, groaning sounds only a camel could make. They knew they would be fed and watered and allowed to rest at the end of a long day's travel before they had to give that night's performance. Each night the camels had to race. This always pleased the people who watched. Huge Reuben rode one camel and the little Philistine ropedancer the other. How funny they looked, perched high, saddleless on the humps—Reuben so large, clinging to the reins, and the ropedancer bouncing about, hanging onto the hump with one hand. The camels had raced so often now that they no longer needed riders, but Nabal thought that having such oddly matched riders made the race more exciting. Reuben and the Philistine threw dice each morning to see which camel would win, but no one who paid to see the race ever seemed the wiser. Although he disliked the camels, Jesse was sometimes sorry for them when they were forced to race the evening after they had traveled long miles along the roads of Israel that day. He was happy when their race was ended and they were permitted a night of peace—almost as happy as when Belshazzar had been permitted his night of rest after his dance.

But would there be rest for old Belshazzar that night too? Had the donkey died along the way to Bethlehem, the boy asked himself in anguish. He had seen dead donkeys lying alone, abandoned, beside the roads of Israel before. As Belshazzar grew older and weaker, Jesse had begun to pity them. Before this he had scarcely noticed the dead animals, the beasts of burden. They had been only vulture's and kite's meat to him. But he had not spied any donkey on the left side of the road, and Saul, who'd moved away to the right, said he hadn't seen one either.

Nabal dismounted and went to talk to the innkeeper whom Malachi, traveling ahead, had scouted out. He was a fussy little man in a woolen robe who kept shrugging his shoulders and then swerving his head to yell at the inn servants, who bustled, half running, about the crowded courtyard. The inn was full, and the innkeeper kept turning travelers away, saying, "I have no space here. I cannot accommodate one more traveler." But wily Nabal did not ask for lodging. No, he'd buy his food for his per-

formers in the market, and his circus had its own
tents. All he asked was his dinner, Malachi's and
the fortuneteller's, and the courtyard and enough
room in which to give his show that night. He would
pay the innkeeper part of what the circus took in
that evening. The innkeeper agreed, of course. Inn-
keepers were usually as greedy as Nabal, every bit
as eager for something for nothing. And they always
complained when the circus owner gave them less
than they expected.

Reuben and the one-eyed man went to buy food
for the performers and meat for the lion while the
boxers threw down hay from the sheaves tied above
King Solomon's cage. Saul and Jesse took buckets
to the well in the center of the courtyard. Their first
task was always to water the animals. Jesse took a
sip of the cold water from his bucket. How wonderful it would be if he could water Belshazzar once
more! By now the donkey would be very thirsty.
The boys watered the circus animals, and by this
time Reuben was back from the market. He tossed
a sack of dried raisins and grain cakes to the other
performers and to the two boys. This was to be
their supper. They would drink water and eat raisins
while Nabal, Malachi and the greatly privileged
fortuneteller went into the inn to drink dark wine
and eat roast goose. To pay for their dinner the
astrologer would tell the innkeeper's future—a glow-
ing one, of course. Jesse's nose quivered. He'd spied

out the fat birds turning golden brown on the spits in the inn kitchen when a servant left the door open wide for an instant. Perhaps if the inn door was left open for a moment, a rather long moment, he could have a bit of goose for himself and for Saul? But he would have to move very swiftly and very carefully. Thinking further, the mute boy discarded the idea as too dangerous. There were too many people about.

Nabal's performers ate with little complaint. They hadn't expected anything better. But Jesse didn't eat. Instead, he stuffed a handful of raisins and two grain cakes into the worn leather pouch that had been his father's. Jesse got up from the courtyard fire. Saul saw his movement. He arose too and came over to follow his friend, who melted into the shadows of some oxcarts. "Where are you going, Jesse?" Saul asked him.

Jesse pointed beyond the courtyard to the street and then walked four fingers along his arm as animals walked.

"Belshazzar?" said Saul quietly. "You're going to try to find the donkey?"

Jesse nodded.

Saul put his hand on the other boy's arm. "Don't do this, Jesse. The white donkey is dead. No, don't look at me that way! I didn't see him beside the road. I told you the truth. But just the same I think he couldn't have made it to Bethlehem."

The mute boy shook his head violently from side to side.

The acrobat sighed and let his hand drop. "So that's what you decided back there on the road? To go find Belshazzar? Go ahead, then. I promised I wouldn't try to stop you. Come back when you find him—or if you don't find him, Jesse. I'm sorry, Jesse. I didn't know you cared that much about old Belshazzar. I guess all I ever really think about nowadays is getting money saved to go to Rome and getting away from Nabal. I'll tell him and Malachi something about your leaving—I don't know what—but I'll tell them. Maybe I'll tell them you're hunting for a fine donkey here you think you can train." Saul's face brightened now. "They'll swallow that idea. I know it."

Jesse took his friend's hand, squeezed it hard once and then moved out into the throng of people who streamed into the inn courtyard, calling loudly and in vain for a place to spend the night.

Saul went sadly back to the fire. Only he had seen Jesse leave. None of the other performers had ever paid much attention to him. The mute boy, like the camels and donkeys, was just there.

As for Jesse, he had known this was how it would be. His absence would scarcely be noticed.

The boy meant to find Belshazzar. He didn't know how he was to do this. He couldn't ask anyone if he'd seen a tall bearded man, a carpenter from

Nazareth, leading an old white donkey. Saul had said the man *was* tall. Even if Jesse could speak, the question would be a laughable one. Bethlehem was full of tall men leading donkeys. It was full of blue-mantled women riding donkeys. Jesse had never known that there were so many donkeys in all Israel. He stood beside the street in the center of the little city watching people stream past him in both directions. How could he ever find Belshazzar?

For twelve agonizing days the mute boy searched for Belshazzar in the moving crowds, but he had no success. There were too many brown-robed men and too many donkeys. Some of the animals looked like Belshazzar through a moment's empty space in the parades of folk who came to Bethlehem. But when Jesse fought his way to them he was always disappointed. The donkeys may have been small and whitish, but they were never the donkey he sought with all his heart.

Jesse ate what he could safely steal, taking more care than usual not to be caught so he would not have to give up the search. And he slept wherever he could find a sheltered place—sometimes under a cart, more often in a doorway where the wind did not sweep down so chill and bone-biting from the hills. The boy didn't worry about Nabal and the people of the circus. It wasn't likely they would come after him. If they wanted to know where he was, Saul could tell them whatever he chose—even the truth, that Jesse ben Abdiel hunted for a donkey that was probably dead. Nabal, Reuben, Malachi, the ropedancer and the one-eyed man would roar with laughter at the foolishness of his quest, but that did not matter to the boy from Arad. He grew all the more thin, and his eyes grew larger in his face. He had a look about him that made people shy away when he approached them. Jesse had some money, only a little, in his pouch, but he would much rather thieve than spend this for food. Stealing in part repaid the people of Bethlehem for taking Belshazzar away from him. He hated the little city of David.

On the evening of the twelfth day Jesse left the city, totally discouraged. He wandered up into the hills that encircled it, weary of folk who stared at him as if he were mad and weary also of noisy, jostling people who always led the wrong white donkeys. Without entirely knowing what he did, Jesse sought the healing silence of the hills—although they were not the hills he had known guarding his uncle's sheep in Arad. He began to climb. He was tired, more tired than he had ever been, and he let himself fall back on the harsh, spiky grass, cropped short by the sheep. A shepherd was somewhere near him, playing his pipes, calling the white, fat-tailed sheep to him to safety for the night. Jesse ben Abdiel knew the melody he played, but his own pipes remained inside his robe. He had no sheep to guard. He had no one!

The boy squeezed his eyes tight shut against the powerful light of the star that seemed to him to stand directly over his head as he rested on the hillside east of the city of David. His head ached, and although he closed his eyes and put his palms over them, he could still see the strange star behind his eyelids. It was every bit as bright as day there in the hills, beside the road, but Jesse, exhausted, fell asleep and dreamed of a lively young Belshazzar, dancing in the great circuses of Rome and receiving a bag of gold from Caesar Augustus himself, while Saul, the famous acrobat, watched, grinning in approval.

Jesse slept while the star moved onward to the city of David and stopped its progress over it, bathing the stone buildings in its brilliant white light. He slept while the bedazzled shepherds with their flocks high in the hills above him cried out in terror when they saw how the star halted its blazing movement. He did not hear the great ringing voice from the skies that spoke to the shepherds, making them leave their sheep and hurry down to Bethlehem. Jesse slept for a long time, and he woke to rub his eyes only when he heard the tinkle of camel bells.

Camel bells meant but one thing to him—Nabal's

circus. Half dazed with sleep, Jesse was confused.
Was Nabal going north to Nazareth so soon? The
boy scrambled to his feet. He didn't want Nabal
to catch him here. The man would drag him along
to tend his camels. That would be the end of Jesse's
search for his donkey.

The road to Bethlehem lay just below Jesse, and
as the mute boy waited, shivering in the cold night
air, wondering if he should hide or not, three white
camels came swaying along it. Jesse blinked in
amazement. Although the camels had very fine
saddles and bridles, quite the finest he had ever
seen, it wasn't the animals that made Jesse not
believe what he saw. He had seen Nabal's camels
every day.

It was the riders who were so surprising. Whoever
they were, they were not of the house of David. He
couldn't begin to guess where they did come from.
The leader was an old man with very white skin,
a high-bridged nose and a long white beard. On
his head he wore a tall black cap with earflaps.
Figures of the sun, moon, stars and comets were
embroidered on it. His cloak was of Tyrian purple,
and under this he had a white robe of heavy cloth
fringed with gold. The second rider had a short
black beard and piercing eyes. On his head he wore
a red hat with a high flat crown. His cloak was of
green wool and his robe of a strangely shimmering
yellow stuff. The last stranger's hair could not be

seen at all because of a large scarlet turban. He had no beard and his skin was so dark that he looked as if he had been baked and burned by the suns of Araby all his life. He wore a long-sleeved garment of blue and over it a cloak, which was the skin of some tawny striped beast.

The only things common to the unusual travelers were their tall white camels and the boots the men wore—of gilded leather, boots that turned up at the toes, boots such as Jesse had never seen before in his life.

As the boy stood open-mouthed, the first rider pulled his camel to a halt. The man pointed to the sleeping city below. "Is this Bethlehem of Judea, lad?" he asked in a soft voice, his accent so very strange that Jesse could scarcely understand him.

Jesse nodded yes, and the man threw three silver coins to the ground at the boy's feet. Then, in an unfamiliar language, he called to his two companions, who urged their camels into a swift trot. The boy knelt wonderingly to pick up the coins. Three staters just for a piece of information! The strangers must be kings if they had so much money to throw to boys they met along the road. They must surely be kings, three kings, he decided. For a long moment Jesse stood to watch as the kings hurried down the hill, their camel's hooves turning the road's dust to drifts of glittering starlit whiteness.

For a moment he forgot Belshazzar and his own

quest. Jesse ben Abdiel followed the three kings as fast as his legs would take him.

The citizens of Bethlehem, the tax gatherers, the Roman soldiers and the visitors had all gone to bed. It was late. The son of Abdiel had slept long. Now for once the city was quiet and the street deserted —no, not quite deserted, for Jesse saw quiet figures, shepherds from the hills, judging from their rough dress of sheepskins, moving too, with the three strangers on camels among them. All kept looking up at the star as if they took their direction from it as they went silently through Bethlehem.

The boy was dizzy. The growing brilliance of the star hurt his head more than ever. It didn't occur to Jesse that it was strange that shepherds left their sheep to prowling wild animals to come into Bethlehem—a thing no good shepherd would ever do. He hurried behind them and went where the odd procession led.

The three stranger kings stopped at an inn not far from the inn where the circus of Nabal was playing, but Jesse didn't think of that. He couldn't think at all. He felt controlled by something he did not understand and he did not question. He must follow the strangers and the shepherds!

This humble courtyard was jammed with travelers also, but they slept now under their carts, wrapped in their cloaks and coverlets. Not a single animal lifted his head to whinny or to snort or bray as the newcomers arrived. Even the beasts slept. The shepherds drifted by the sleepers on noiseless feet, and then the kings made their camels kneel while they dismounted. Not one of the white camels groaned in typical camel fashion. No one awakened to wonder at the remarkable appearance of the richly dressed strangers or to ask why shepherds left their flocks.

Jesse stood in the deepest shadows he could find. He felt fear clutch at him. What was happening here? He wanted to run away, but something held him still. He had to find out what drew these people to this particular inn so late at night. The oldest king gestured wordlessly at the star and then bowed his head as if he worshiped. The other two kings, each in turn, did the same thing, while the star, as bright as a white sun, shed its light on them. The terrible star seemed to focus its rays chiefly on the little inn. Each line of the roof, each stairway was picked out with silvery white. The star filled the courtyard well with its blazing reflection. It was beautiful—and frightening.

Jesse held his breath, watching the kings from his hiding place as each stranger took a box from the breast of his magnificent robe. Then they strode forward in single file, walking behind the white-bearded, purple-robed leader. The boy followed, lost in curiosity and in wonder. Through an archway the shepherds and kings wound their way to the stables of the inn. And still the boy, unnoticed by them, followed in their footsteps.

A little shepherd, younger than Jesse, opened a creaking old wooden door and called out softly to other shepherds who stood waiting outside. "In here! *They're* in here. I found them. Come, see!" He held the door open as the shepherds and the kings went into the stable. Last of all came the son of Abdiel. What possibly could be in this stable? Jesse's nose, by now very accustomed to such things, told him at once that the innkeeper's hay was cheap and moldy and that the animals' water was brackish. This wasn't a very good stable. Why would people come here? Simple shepherds, perhaps—but "kings," certainly not!

The boy stood on his tiptoes to see, wondering if everyone, including himself, had been driven to madness by the star. Luckily the shepherd who stood in front of him was shorter than he was. Jesse had a good view and stared about him. The star's light did not penetrate here, yet the stable was bathed in a lovely yellow color, one far more gentle than that of the star. Amazed, Jesse watched the three kings fall on their knees before one of the mangers. The hay had been taken out of it, and in the place of the fodder lay a baby, a very new baby, wrapped in white cloth. A woman with long brown hair, a woman with a calmly beautiful face, a woman dressed in a blue mantle and white gown, sat above the child, smiling down at him. Behind her stood a tall man in a plain brown robe. The soft light fell on them and on the baby in a pure shaft of golden light.

Jesse gasped. It was *the* man! The man who had bought Belshazzar! This was all the boy could think of. Jesse had come out of his strange dreamlike state the moment he had seen the man in the brown robe. He quickly looked away from the people crowded around the manger. People lodging in a stable? What a strange thing. But where was *his* donkey? Where was Belshazzar?

The boy didn't bother to look on while the kings put their gifts, gold and the costly spices frankincense and myrrh, worshipfully before the woman and the baby. He closed his ears to the wondering murmur of the shepherds, who had never seen such a sight. The boy's nose twitched a little when he smelled the fragrance of the frankincense, but that was all. He slipped easily in and out among the shepherds, who did not take notice of him.

Jesse had found what he had sought for twelve long days. Belshazzar, Jesse's Belshazzar, stood with other donkeys, some cows and a goat, staring at the baby in the manger. The donkey looked so wise and thoughtful that for a moment Jesse was unsure it was the right animal, but then Belshazzar tweaked an ear forward in a special way only he had, and Jesse knew he had found his donkey. The boy slid

behind everyone in the stable. Now his hand found
Belshazzar's rope and, unseen by the shepherds or
by the three kings, he silently led Belshazzar away.
He did not mark the woman's soft blue-green eyes
as she watched him. She had turned her head away
from her child for only a moment, and then she
looked back down at the baby and smiled. She
made no sound of protest. She had lifted her hand
for only a moment as the boy and donkey left—
something no one else had seen as they gave their
attention to the baby.

The stable door was still ajar. Jesse had been
afraid it would creak when he opened it, but luck
was with him. He led Belshazzar out into the night.
There in the courtyard behind the stable he flung
his arms around the donkey's neck. Then, in spite
of his great joy, the greatest he had ever known,
Jesse ben Abdiel noticed something odd. His eyes
no longer hurt him.

The great star over Bethlehem—the star that had
shown in the heavens for many days—had at last
begun to dim.

VI. JERUSALEM

The boy made his way, leading the donkey, through the archway, across the courtyard where the travelers and animals still slept their strange sleep, and out onto the road that led away from the little city. Swiftly Jesse and Belshazzar passed through Bethlehem, the road under their feet changing from silver-white to pale gray as the star faded more and more and the moon took its rightful place in the sky. Now it was another night world, one that Jesse was more at home in. He looked up at the half-moon gratefully, then pulled his robe closer

92

about his shoulders and clicked his tongue at the donkey to hurry. Jesse wanted to be as far away from the city of David as possible before dawn. The two of them would hide among the boulders by the day, far from the side of the busy road. No one would find them there. The carpenter from Nazareth had only bought the donkey to carry his wife to Bethlehem, hadn't he? What further use did he have for Belshazzar?

The boy took the road that led north—to Jerusalem, the city he had bypassed so often but had never entered. Jerusalem was a great city. He could hide himself and Belshazzar there, but now his plan went no farther than this—getting to Jerusalem.

To Jesse's relief, Belshazzar came along easily at the pace he set. It was very strange, though. Something had happened to the little white donkey, Jesse thought—something very, very strange. The moment he thought they were far enough from Bethlehem, Jesse turned to examine Belshazzar. The moonlight was not as bright by any means as the strange star, but it was bright enough to let the boy see Belshazzar well. Although the red harness was gone, the donkey looked the same, but he no longer shuffled. He was strong again, although his muzzle was still white, more white with age than the rest of him. Jesse looked into Belshazzar's eyes, and the donkey met the boy's gaze calmly and almost sadly. It *was* Belshazzar, of course, but somehow he wasn't quite the same donkey—not even the sick animal of the road to Bethlehem twelve days past. The eyes had changed. Jesse was uneasy. He felt for the old scar on the side of Belshazzar's neck, a relic of one of the donkey's many battles with other animals. Yes, it was there, and the other scar, the very large one made by a horse's teeth, was on the donkey's flank.

The boy scratched his head in wonder. Then he snapped his fingers. Of course. That was it! The man from Nazareth had given the old donkey a tonic or some sort of medicine that Jesse didn't know about. After all, the carpenter and his wife did come from Galilee, and Galileans were strange people, who might know of herbs that grew only in their province of Israel. Jesse had often heard of such strange potions in the circus. Whatever it was the carpenter had given the donkey would wear off, and Belshazzar would be himself again, the circus performer. Then Jesse thought further. But if it wore off, would the donkey be ill again? But what had the carpenter dosed the donkey with that made him change so?

They trudged along under the moon until Jesse saw the first lines of light in the east. It was time for them to get away and hide now. He led the donkey down a path into a ravine, one with a small brook at its bottom and sycamore trees on its sides. They shielded the floor of the ravine from the view of passersby on the road above. There was a patch of yellowish grass near the brook, and Belshazzar, his rope trailing, ambled over to drink from it while Jesse ate what he had stolen the night before from a baker's shop. The three staters the kings had given him would be needed in Jerusalem, he had already decided. He took them out and looked at them in the palm of his hand. Although three staters wasn't such a huge sum of money, it was an amazing amount to give just for a piece of information—just to answer one question. The three men were clearly mad. They had been kneeling before the baby in the stable as if he were a king. A king in a stable? Jesse laughed, and Belshazzar lifted his head to look mildly at the boy. It was all crazy, Jesse thought, but it did not concern him now that he had Belshazzar back. He whistled to the donkey to come to him, and Belshazzar came shambling over the grass.

Jesse was pleased with himself. As the morning sun rose over the brow of one of the hills that sheltered the ravine, the boy and donkey fell fast asleep, Jesse's head pillowed on Belshazzar's familiar warm shaggy hide.

They traveled again by night, making good time, seen by almost no one. Like smoke, the boy and the donkey drifted through slumbering nameless villages. Two hours after dawn of the second day, they arrived at a great gate of Jerusalem, the selfsame Gate of Ephraim where Jesse had stood months

before when he had first come from Arad. A ragged
boy and an old white donkey weren't strange sights
in Jerusalem. Exactly as Jesse had guessed, no one
paid attention to them. The guards at the gate,
resplendent in their helmets and cloaks, didn't flick a
suspicious eyelid as the pair went into the city. People in Jerusalem were too busy with their own affairs,
making a profit from the pilgrims who came constantly to the temple, to take much notice of other
people. There were always many pilgrims in the
city, for it was a law of the Jews that no Jew could
live more than ninety days' journey from the temple.
That meant that the people of Israel came often to
worship and to bring sacrifices of lambs and doves
to the priests. Jesse had learned very well in Bethlehem how difficult it was to find something or
someone in a moving crowd. The largest city in
Israel was the safest place he knew for a thief and
a stolen donkey. In the throngs of Jerusalem the
carpenter, even if he passed through the great city
of Herod on his way home to Nazareth in the north,
would not easily find his white donkey.

By now Jesse had eaten the last of his food. He
was hungry, and he knew the donkey was hungry,
too. Belshazzar's appetite had come back, even if
he no longer playfully nipped at his master as he
once had done. Jesse spent one of his staters for
food, but to save money he and the donkey went
out into the countryside to sleep. The boy was

uneasy under a roof. His months with Nabal's circus had made him feel like this, but still he wished for a tent and was often cold at night. He missed Saul badly. He had no one to speak for him. Jesse knew he would have to find work soon. There was one thing that would quickly earn him money—a good deal of money, but it was the one thing Belshazzar must not do: dance! Some visitor or pilgrim to Jerusalem might recognize the donkey and see Nabal somewhere else someday. Nabal would certainly ferret out the white donkey and get him back if he knew that Belshazzar was able to perform again. It wouldn't matter to the circus master that he had sold the animal to the carpenter. Nabal would consider getting Belshazzar back and also keeping the carpenter's money a piece of remarkably good fortune.

The temple, the great temple of Jerusalem drew the boy like a lure when he could finally screw his courage up to it. He had to go there, to the center of the Hebrew world, although he did not expect to find work there. He stood before it, his jaw dropping, as he gawked at the towering walls and huge gates. He found the courage only once to enter by the Golden Gate into the huge Court of Gentiles, where anyone could go. The din and confusion there made him want to run away. The cries of the sellers of sacrificial doves, beautiful white birds held captive in wooden cages, made the boy's ears ring, as did the shouts of the money changers, who, for a fee, would give Jewish coins for any money known in the world—Roman, Greek, Phoenician, Persian, anything. Jesse edged away from the pens where the sheep were imprisoned, also waiting to be sold and sacrificed on the altar. The sight of the pitiful bleating animals upset him, as any sight of brutality to beasts now did, but still he could not tear himself away from the temple. A kind-faced old woman said that she would watch his donkey for him to see that no one stole it if he wished to go into another court—as far as he could go as a Jewish boy but not yet as a man.

How he gazed at the knots of men dressed in long dark gowns, clustering around a very old man with a long beard who spoke to them while they hung onto every word. Little did Jesse ben Abdiel realize that he had seen Hillel, the greatest of the Jerusalem rabbis. He could even have listened to him, but at that moment the high priest, dressed in beautifully embroidered robes, his black beard waist-length, came striding by surrounded by a throng of yellow-gowned, beardless Levites. Jesse had stood amazed for a long time, gazing about him, until he heard the thunderous noise of the huge bronze Nicanor Gate being shut in the Court of Men. He did not know that it took twenty men to open it, but the sound so terrified him that he fled back to the Court of Gentiles to grab Belshazzar's halter and hurry with him out of the temple. Twice the throngs nearly parted him and the donkey and buffeted the frail boy against the wall, between a money changer's table and a high column. Breaking free, boy and donkey charged wildly through the crowds still pushing to get inside the temple walls although it was nearly evening and the silver trumpets would soon sound the last sacrifice and the end of the day. Jesse leaned, breathless, against the wall of the Antonia, the tall fortlike palace the Romans occupied with their soldiers, officers and officials. For a moment he leaned there, and then he saw two legionaries, fair-skinned, fair-haired men, coming down the narrow street directly toward him. They were Gauls who had taken service in the legions of Rome, and they meant no harm to Jesse, but the boy didn't know that. He took one look at their strange faces, jerked at Belshazzar's halter again and fled from the four-towered grim palace that housed the unclean heathen Roman rulers. Jesse had heard Nabal's fortuneteller speak more than once of the impurity of the Romans and say that under no circumstances would he, a Jew, enter a Roman house to tell a fortune—no matter how many pieces of gold he was given.

That night the boy often trembled as he slept in the hills. Jerusalem was a frightening place, but here he must stay for safety. It did not occur to him for a whole day that he had left no offering of money at the temple—but what did he have to offer? He needed what little he had.

Hopefully the boy went to other places in the city, along the narrow winding streets and up and down the many stairways that led to the section of the merchants and to the upper town where the rich lived. He went hurriedly by the white marble palace of Herod, king of Israel, averting his eyes. He feared Herod. Nabal and Malachi had said that he, the king, was a disgrace to his people, a man who built theaters and hippodromes to give plays like a Greek and to race horses like a Roman. The boy knew Herod was a friend to the heathen. He had had ten wives, one after another, and he had had his sons murdered. Jesse shuddered just to think of it. It was true enough that Herod built palaces and made the city squares wider, but what of that? What of the fact that Herod built the great temple? Jesse had heard the other tales too—that the king wandered about Jerusalem, unknown and unrecognized, asking unsuspecting people what they thought of Herod the Great. The man who told the inquiring stranger the truth far too often mysteriously disappeared.

Jesse believed the streets of the guilds—the little streets where the dyers, fullers, sandalmakers, goldsmiths and others congregated—would be the place to find someone willing to hire him and Belshazzar to transport his goods. But no, each merchant had his own donkey or mule. There was no need for

Belshazzar's services. Then, the boy tried the famous Pool of Siloam. Perhaps the people who came there would want to be carried to their homes. But no, they did not. They were poor folk too, and they always walked.

For four days the boy and donkey went up and down Jerusalem searching for work, each day growing more hungry, Jesse each day growing more desperate. He did not dare thieve in this city. He remembered all too well why Nabal and the circus had been expelled from Jerusalem. He remembered the talk of the old juggler who was crucified for stealing. He could not leave the sanctuary of Jerusalem, but he could easily starve there, too. The smell of evening food being cooked drifting out of the windows of the stone houses nauseated him. The swift terror-stricken detours he made with Belshazzar when they saw Herod's swaggering soldiers in their black cloaks or Romans in their red ones made his heart pound and the donkey's sides heave. The "city of the high place" was a cruel one, the boy from Arad decided.

Jesse's dumbness had been hard to bear before. Now it almost maddened him. No one understood him. People shoved him out of the way when he tried to appeal to them by gestures and by making faces, the only things a mute could do. They thought the ragged boy was a beggar. Jerusalem, a city of open-handed pilgrims, had far too many beggars already. Once, on the third day, Jesse had an inspiration. He approached one of the public letter writers who strolled in a square of the city near the temple, his ink, his reed and papyrus carried along with him. Perhaps if the scribe would write something for Jesse about a "strong willing boy" and a "strong willing donkey" wanting work? A piece of papyrus with this message would make things easier. A great many Jews could read—read far better than he could. Then they would know that the son of Abdiel was no beggar. He would have to pay the scribe to write this, of course. He had a coin remaining—one he had refused to spend so far. If only the boy could make the letter writer know what he wanted. The scribe was not unpleasant, but he did not seem to understand what Jesse needed. He asked many questions once he realized that the boy could hear and understand, but Jesse could only make motions with his hands and shake his tousled black head. The scribe went on asking patiently. Did Jesse wish to write his family saying he was in Jerusalem? Did Jesse wish to ask something of the priests in the temple? For some reason the scribe thought Jesse was an apprentice on an errand for his master or a runaway slave. It was hopeless. Finally, both gave up in disgust and in sadness. The letter writer walked away to the temple shaking his head while a bitterly unhappy Jesse stalked off the other way, glowering, followed by Belshazzar. If only Saul had been with him! Jesse thought often of Saul. Where was he? When would the circus bypass Jerusalem on its way north to Nazareth? How he wished he could have even one glimpse of Saul. He was so lonely he would even have enjoyed seeing Reuben or the one-eyed man again. The boy grew more and more desperate. He haunted the marketplaces, as his best hope, but no one asked him to hire out his donkey to carry leeks, sacks of dry lentils, baskets of fowl or anything else. He sat at the gates of the city, meeting the merchants who came into Jerusalem with what they had to sell. He would even work for the felt-hatted Greeks, heathens, or nose-ringed Babylonian merchants. But no one asked him to carry goods for him. Each person he sought out either misunderstood him or had his own pack animal.

At sunset of the fifth day Jesse walked along in despair toward the gate that led out to the northern hills where he and Belshazzar would sleep. But before he reached that gate, he noticed an old woman in a dirty shawl sitting with her back against the wall of a house, her hands folded across her plump stomach. Jesse knew who she was. She was Jaala. He'd seen her about the city often enough. She was a potseller, and what a voice she had for selling her wares. She could even outshout the strong young water vendors. No one could shut out her cries: "Pots! Fine strong pots! Who'll buy Jaala's pots today?"

As she walked along she pushed before her a

rickety two-wheeled cart filled with painted and unpainted pots. It looked like hard work for such an old woman, and Jesse had seen how she eyed Belshazzar and him when she had met them in the city. Now her eyes were fixed on the boy's face. They were sharp little eyes, black like a tortoise's. Her voice was as sharp as her glance. "Are you hungry, boy?" she demanded.

Jesse shook his head, lying.

"Well, answer me when I ask you a question!" She was angry.

Jesse shook his head and, hating as always the usual gestures of a mute, once more pointed to his lips and then put his hand behind his ear.

The old woman understood this time. "Oho!" she shrilled. "So you're dumb, you are? Is that donkey yours, or did you steal him? I'll wager you're a thief. All boys are thieves, aren't they?"

The question was unanswerable and not truly fair. Jesse hadn't been a thief in Arad. He didn't know what to do—so he did nothing. He only looked at the potseller.

"Well, no mind what you are or where that donkey came from," Jaala cackled. "Makes no difference to me. Do you want to work for me? Mind you, I can't pay you, but you can live in my house, and I'll feed you. The taxes I pay make me poor. You both look starved. I'm a poor woman, as I have said, but I do have a house in this city."

Jesse was amazed at his good luck. At the moment he didn't care if he got paid or not. He nodded again and again while the old woman got to her feet and took up the handles of her cart. "Come along with me," she ordered. "Tomorrow you and your beautiful donkey will help me sell my pots." She cackled with laughter and glanced over her shoulder at Belshazzar, making fun of him. "There are some old pieces of leather in my courtyard. Can you make a harness for his back? That rope halter he has will do well enough to haul him along with."

The boy nodded. He and Belshazzar followed Jaala up a steep hill and into a tiny courtyard filled with more pots, dozens of them of all shapes and sizes. The woman showed the boy his little room with a tiny lean-to stable next to it. That evening Jesse tried to sleep under the roof of old Jaala's house, but at midnight he gave it up, and taking the dirty flea-filled mat she had given him, he went out into the lean-to and slept next to Belshazzar. Before Jaala was up and about, however, he was back in his room.

For the next few weeks the boy and donkey helped the old potseller peddle her wares in the city, Belshazzar harnessed to her old cart with Jesse leading him while the woman went on ahead shouting for folk to buy her fine pots. Jesse didn't like Jaala. She never struck him or his donkey, but she had a cruel tongue and often poked fun at his and Belshazzar's

appearance. Nothing that Jesse did suited her. She
didn't overfeed him or the donkey either, although
she had plenty for herself. The worst thing about the
woman was her constant grumbling and scolding.
Jesse came to believe that she hired him and Belshazzar because neither of them could answer her
back when she cursed them for stupidity or laziness.
The boy had peace and quiet only when the potseller went to the temple to worship, and she went
there seldom, because she had to make an offering
of money or sacrificial animals there. Jaala did not
want to part with one lepton if she could keep it.
Mostly she sat under a tattered awning on her flat
rooftop, muttering about the injustices of the world
and the three husbands who had disappointed her
by dying before she did so she must continue to
work.

And then one evening while they were going up
a steep hill, Jesse and Belshazzar's good fortune
deserted them. The donkey slipped on the slick
cobblestones. He fell to his knees first, but then
toppled over until he lay at full length. Jesse was
terrified. The donkey's newfound strength seemed
to be leaving him. Jesse had first noticed it two
weeks past. Perhaps it was because he wasn't getting enough to eat at Jaala's house? Belshazzar had
never taken up his old habits of biting and kicking
—the habits he'd had when Jesse had first known
him—but for a time he'd held his head high. But

recently it had begun to sag again as it had on the road to Bethlehem, forty days before, and he showed less affection for the boy than he'd shown for many days.

Jesse was at Belshazzar's side in a moment, trying to get the makeshift harness he had made off the donkey while Jaala screamed in anger. Her cart had tipped over and some of her pots were smashed. She blamed the donkey. "Your dirty old beast broke my best pots!" she yelled at Jesse as the boy got the harness off. "Get out of my sight, you two. Don't you ever come back to my house!"

She shouted so loudly that Jesse and the donkey both escaped down the street, her curses floating after them.

Hopelessly, the boy followed after the stumbling animal, who had got up with Jesse's tugging help. What were they going to do now?

Jesse did not catch up with Belshazzar's headlong flight. At the bottom of the sloping street, the donkey paused in full view of his master. All at once he began to bray so loudly that Jesse gritted his teeth and put his fingers into his ears. He had thought old Jaala was loud, and he had known Belshazzar could be very, very noisy, but not so noisy as this. Where did he get the strength? Then, as the boy watched the white donkey, surprised at his peculiar behavior, he saw Belshazzar shoot forward at a gallop around a corner. The boy plunged after him, but stopped short at what he saw. He ducked behind a corner of a house, not wanting to be spied out.

What terrible luck!

There in the little square of fullers stood Belshazzar, rubbing his head fondly against a man's sleeve, a thing the donkey had done only to Jesse. It was the tall man in brown homespun the donkey was favoring. The woman in the blue mantle, her baby in her arms, stood beside him, smiling.

"Why it *is* the donkey we bought. See these scars where he's been badly treated. I remember them all," an envious Jesse heard the carpenter say to his wife in his deep gentle voice. "We've found our old donkey again. He'll take us away just as he took us into Bethlehem."

Totally crushed by what he'd seen Belshazzar do, the mute boy didn't wait to hear more. What did it matter to him now? Belshazzar had *wanted* to go to those people. That was why the white donkey had brayed so loudly. The donkey had chosen them —not Jesse. Belshazzar was happier with the carpenter than with him.

Jesse knew when he was beaten. He walked away, dejected, from the couple from Nazareth, his eyes on his feet, not once looking back. Alone, he'd look for work again tomorrow, but today he didn't have the heart to hear anyone else say "no" to him. Belshazzar had just said the most terrible "no" of all. Something had changed between Jesse and the dancing donkey since Belshazzar had been with the man from Nazareth. Jesse had sensed it often, but had not known what it was. But now he did. It was very simple. The donkey didn't return his love any more. The boy blinked back tears. He felt in his father's old pouch—not that he really needed to do this. The last stater the oldest king had thrown him lay lonely in it—the stater he had expected to give the letter writer. It would buy Jesse a good supper and a decent place to sleep. The next day he'd make the rounds of the many mule, donkey and camel markets of the city of Herod. He hadn't gone to those places before. He had thought of it when he first came into the city, but he'd known how the knowledgeable men and boys in the animal markets would laugh at Belshazzar, such a sorry-looking donkey. Jesse could not have stood that. Now he need not worry about their laughter. No one laughed at ragged and hungry children, alone, in Herod's city. No one noticed them.

The boy went in the direction of the Damascus Gate, where the animal markets were. There were many inns there that were not costly. He'd heard travelers and pilgrims speak of them. Perhaps if he was lucky he would hear of some merchant who needed a likely lad who knew something of animals, a boy who could curry and calm down even the most stubborn, vicious beast. How Jesse wished he knew what the carpenter from Nazareth had given Belshazzar to make the donkey temporarily well again! What a great secret that would be for an animal handler! The lucky boy who learned that secret would be in great demand and soon a very rich man.

Jesse went into a small tavern near the Damascus Gate, the gate that led to the north. There weren't many people there. It was the wrong hour for the evening meal. The peach-colored evening was past and the banks of sunset clouds had blown away toward the sea. Only two men sat a wooden table across the small bare room. They were eating olives, fish and wheat porridge. Jesse took careful notice of their food, and when the tavern maid came to him, he pointed wordlessly to their wooden dishes and nodded. Yes, he would have the same.

While he waited, Jesse listened, hoping they would give him some hint of where to look for work, but instead one of them began to speak of the over-high price of camels from Araby being brought to Jerusalem. Their conversation was not interesting, and Jesse was about to give up hope. He was even seriously considering becoming a beggar, a thought that would have disgusted him before. There were dozens of mute beggars in Jerusalem, and if there were so many beggars, it couldn't be such an unprofitable trade after all. But the

thought didn't much appeal to him. Of course, now
he could leave Jerusalem, but where would he go?
Back to Nabal, back to Saul? But where was the
circus now?

The boy worried, hunched over his supper, but
when he heard one of the men ask a question of the
other, he gripped his spoon tight. The speaker was
a fat man in a stained light-green robe, a Persian
silk robe. His beard was gray and straggling, but
Jesse recognized him as one of the richest camel
dealers in the city. The boy had seen him two or
three times in the days he'd been in Jerusalem. Old
Jaala had known him and had always greeted him
very respectfully as "Master Caleb."

"By the way, Jonas, what news do you have of the
three strangers from the east you sent me some time
ago?" asked Master Caleb. "I thank both you and
Herod, your master, for that favor. Indeed I do, and
I'll pay you both your profit from that sale soon.
It will be a handsome one, believe me. I sold those
rich strangers my finest white camels, magnificent
animals newly come from the desert, and they didn't
quibble about the price. They were in a great hurry
to leave Jerusalem."

The other man was tiny. His eyes were deep-set
and filmed, and his hands small and clawlike, but
his robe was of scarlet wool and embroidered with
gold thread. There was silver worked into the leather
of his sandals, and the odor of nard, the most costly

of scents, hung about him. "Not so loud, Caleb," the little man named Jonas hissed at his companion. "It is not wise to speak of those three too openly." He lowered his voice while Jesse tilted his head to hear better as if he had found something wrong with his porridge. "Herod is very angry. Didn't anyone ever tell you about the wise men, or are you too busy with your fine camels to listen?"

"I was in southern Judea for a time buying mules," the camel merchant said. "I do not know all of the news, it seems."

The little man bent over the table. "The wise men came to King Herod first of all—which shows that they certainly can't have been so very wise after all. They'd followed that great white star all the way to Israel. They are powerful magicians—or this is what they are supposed to be—from faraway lands to the east."

"What did they want with Herod, Jonas?" Caleb was as curious as Jesse was.

"They were looking for the 'King of Kings'— imagine that? I was there when Herod gave audience to them. They said that they had learned from studying the heavens that the King of Kings was coming soon. Herod was afraid to insult them—such powerful men. He believed that they were magicians and sorcerers, and everyone, even he, saw how richly they were dressed in fine silks and Tyrian-purple garments so fine that even Caesar Augustus in Rome might not own such raiment. They could put an evil spell on Herod, and he didn't want that. Life under the pagan Romans is hard enough without evil spells from strangers. Too, the strangers from the east carried letters to him from the Roman governors of the lands they passed through. That made a difference, all right, a big difference. I could see clearly that Herod was afraid of them. A palace chamberlain like myself gets to know even kings well. We palace servants learn much if we keep our eyes and ears open."

The merchant, fascinated, whispered hoarsely, "Go on, Jonas, my friend."

"Of course, Herod would not like the strangers' talk of *another* king in Israel. He's jealous of his throne, as you know. But he sent for his priests to humor the magicians. The priests told the wise men that the holy books of Israel said that the King of Kings would be found in Bethlehem here in Judea. Of course, as educated men, we have heard that old tale all too often. Herod only wanted his priests to show up well before the strangers from the east."

The camel seller's jaw dropped. "The Messiah! Did they seek the Messiah?" he breathed. "Is that who they wanted?"

Jesse now dropped his spoon into his porridge as he listened.

"Perhaps," Jonas went on. "But I doubt if you have any more faith than I do in the coming of the

Messiah. That is neither here nor there. I personally believe that it is never to be at all. Only country fools, women and children believe nowadays. But let us not speak of Messiahs. We have seen enough of Messiahs here in Jerusalem—dozens of them. Herod sent the three strangers to Bethlehem to find this 'promised king.' The magicians believed that the king could be an infant and that he would be born under that great white star that made us sleep so badly before it disappeared—the Eternal be thanked for its departure. The wise fools believed that he would be born where that star stopped. Did you ever hear such idiotic talk in your life? They were *chasing* that star! Herod made the wise men promise, and you never heard such honeyed words from him before, to come back and tell *him* where this king could be found. I almost laughed at what came next." Jonas, enjoying his story, paused and took a mouthful of hot porridge.

"What came next?" asked Caleb.

"Herod said *he* would go worship the new king, too, when he was found."

"Ha! *I* haven't seen my white camels in Jerusalem since I sold them to the three men from the east," said the merchant with a laugh as he picked up his piece of fish again.

"Of course not," Jonas scoffed. "The strangers weren't complete fools. I said they were supposed to be great sorcerers, didn't I? That takes some kind of talent. They knew our King Herod. Who does not? Imagine Herod worshiping anyone but himself or bowing down before anyone but the Romans? The wise men never came back to Jerusalem. They went back to their own land, and who knows what and where that is? I personally think, after having seen them, that they came from three different lands and that they scattered to go to their homelands. Who knows where they are today? I never expect to see the like of them again!"

Caleb was very pleased. He laughed over his food. "Oh, this is fine. What a story, indeed! Does Herod think the King of Kings will be found? Did Herod chase the star, too? How Herod must hate this! He must hate the thought of another king in the land. Herod finds it bad enough that the Romans only let him pretend to be a king. What will he do now?"

"Be very glad, my friend Caleb, that your sons are all nearly grown men but as yet unmarried—and that you are not a grandsire," warned Jonas, darkly.

"Why? What do my two sons have to do with what I just asked you?"

"Only this." Jonas gestured with the dagger he had used to cut his fish. "Herod has already given his orders. Within three days his soldiers will hunt down every boy child in the land under the age of two years and kill him." The man's voice was a bloodcurdling whisper.

Jesse felt terror grip him as with a clatter he

dropped his own dagger to the tile floor of the tavern. He didn't eavesdrop any more as the camel merchant raised his hands high to protest that not even Herod would dare do such a frightful thing in Israel.

Jonas calmed Caleb down, calling for wine, and then, as Jesse ate, the palace chamberlain looked suspiciously at the boy who had dropped and retrieved a dagger. Jesse bent to his porridge and fish and finished quickly. The men must not suspect that he'd overheard them. Letting his dagger fall had been stupid and had attracted attention, but the boy couldn't leave his supper uneaten, not knowing when he'd have another half so fine. Moreover, if he went out suddenly, the men would be even more suspicious. The tables were a good distance apart. Few people had the mute boy's remarkable ears, but still Jesse wondered if they had guessed he had eavesdropped.

While the boy ate his thoughts raced. The Messiah! The three "kings," the kings he had seen, the baby born in the stable in Bethlehem! Jesse had seen that baby. It was only an ordinary baby. The kings had gone mad. That was why they gave that baby gifts. Jesse thought he knew why Herod's spies had learned nothing. The people in the city of David acted as if they had been drugged into sleep that strange night. Perhaps they were—drugged by the fatigue that had grown worse night after night, the weariness caused by lack of sleep thanks to the blazing star. The same star that probably had maddened the kings. They would have seen nothing. The shepherds would have been back in the hills with their sheep when Herod's men came to ask them questions. Moreover, shepherds were famous in Israel for refusing to talk to folk who wanted to get information from them. The wise men had left Israel without seeing Herod again.

Jesse almost shook his head, but he felt Jonas' eyes flick over to him again and again, so the boy kept his head down. Jesse ben Abdiel thrust away the thought, the ridiculous thought, that this baby could be the King of Kings—the son of a carpenter from Nazareth. Impossible! What Jonas and the rabbi in Arad had said about the Messiah was the right thing to hold to. Abdiel, Jesse's father, had only suffered for his belief, and had been called a fool and a dreamer, and people had said more than once that Abdiel had a demon in him. This would not be said of the son of Abdiel.

One strong thought came out of all of the boy's hasty reflections. The baby was in terrible danger— and if that baby was in danger, so was Belshazzar, who now traveled with the family from Nazareth. There was no mistaking what the carpenter had said to his wife in the square of the fullers. They were going away, leaving Jerusalem. And the man from Herod's palace had said that within three days

Herod's own soldiers, his many men in black cloaks, would start to murder throughout the land of Israel. I must do something, Jesse told himself in mounting panic. He threw his last stater on the table and waited fearfully, trying to pretend an interest in the wall in front of him so he would not catch the palace chamberlain's eye again until the tavern maid brought him some copper coins. Then he shoveled them off into his purse and left the inn.

Jesse strolled out innocently and slowly, sensing that Jonas watched him still, but once around the corner and out of sight, the boy began to run out of the Damascus Gate quarter of Jerusalem as swiftly as his feet would take him. The carpenter, the man from Nazareth, his wife and baby son were leaving Jerusalem. Belshazzar was leaving with them.

Even if the donkey no longer loved Jesse, Jesse loved him!

VII. THE JOPPA GATE

As fast as his feet would take him, Jesse ben Abdiel ran through the city to the little square where he had last seen Belshazzar. As he ran he remembered that there had been someone else who witnessed the tender scene between the white donkey and the tall carpenter. A beggar had sat cross-legged before one of the fuller's shops. If Jesse was lucky, the beggar might still be there.

And so he was, sitting exactly as the boy had last seen him, his begging bowl in his lap. The man whined when the boy stopped in front of him. "Alms,

119

alms for the poor. I have not eaten since the Sabbath."

Jesse threw a small coin into the bowl. He squatted down and then as quickly as his fingers could move he sketched four figures in the dust, a donkey, a man, a woman and a baby. Then he stood and pointed to the four directions one after another.

For a wonder the toothless old beggar understood at once. "The man in the brown robe and the woman with the baby they'd brought to the temple? Ah yes, I remember them well. They gave me twice as much as you have done." The man looked down at his bowl. This time it was Jesse who understood. Reluctantly he put another coin into the bowl. Now the beggar would speak again. "I heard what they said. They leave Jerusalem. They go to the sea; they leave Israel. I was not meant to hear, but I could not stop my ears—not with these." He showed the boy stumps of hands and cackled with laughter. "I was born so, but I tell people it is a punishment of the pagan Romans for cursing them too loudly. It makes men give me alms when they think the Romans cut off my hands. Go to the Joppa Gate, whoever you are. You could be in time to find them if you hurry." He glanced into his pottery bowl and sniffed. He did not say "May the Eternal be merciful to you" as Jesse darted away. The shock-haired, burning-eyed boy had not given him that much money.

Jesse hastened to the west of the city now. He knew the Joppa Gate. He had stood beneath it often enough with Belshazzar when they had first come to Jerusalem. But would he be in time? The boy dodged expertly by some Greeks in amethyst-colored and saffron-hued tunics with gold dust in their hair. The scent of cassia and anise hung about them as they went down, laughing, into a cellar tavern, but Jesse moved so swiftly by them that he did not even smell it. All he could think of was the donkey he loved.

Now the Joppa Gate lay just ahead of him. Its three huge towers, lit by blazing torches stuck in metal sconces in the wall, loomed forbiddingly above him. The boy looked about him wildly. A caravan of mules laden with dried fruit, salt fish and great jars of olive oil waited to leave. Behind it a dealer in horses, a Bedouin by his dress of goat-hair cloth and head covering, stood with a dozen horses, beautiful horses from Araby with long manes and tails, flashing eyes and small heads—swift desert horses. The leader of the caravan from Israel went on arguing with Jerusalem merchants as his caravan waited to permit another, one from the west, to file through the inner gate. The mules of the second caravan carried bales of cloth, silks from Persia, baskets of glassware from Sidon, while its dozen haughty camels had been laden with hampers of Lebanese iron. Eight donkeys stepped along behind the camels. On their backs were bags of light but precious stuff, spices and sandalwood. Except for the two caravans the huge space before the inner gate was deserted.

Where was Belshazzar? Was Jesse too late?

In agony the boy waited, biting at his knuckles. He'd wait for a short time, he decided, but not for long. If the carpenter and his family didn't come soon, he'd go out alone onto the western road. Jesse ben Abdiel had nothing worth stealing. He owned nothing but his dagger and his shepherd's pipes, which were close to worthless. He had lost his staff long weeks ago. The boy wasn't afraid of the many bandits who infested the roads of Israel—perhaps he'd even join them if they asked him. Jesse sank down on his heels in the shadows. Herod's city guards and the Roman guards who shared their watch paid no attention to him. They stared straight ahead. Not even the caravan leader's screeching at the merchants as he tried to force them to raise his pay affected the soldiers. Jesse knew caravan leaders. They were outcasts in Israel. Some of them were even in league with bandits. This leader would be no different from the others, the boy guessed. Now Jesse heard something swell over the man's shouting —the sound of voices, many voices. He sank farther back into the blackness of the Joppa Gate as a group of people, travelers and pilgrims returning home, came up to the waiting caravan. Jesse knew that they hoped to go with it—to band together for protection. Their leader, a man in a gray-blue robe, now began to shout at the caravan leader, too. At last all was settled, and the leader and his helpers, ragged lads Jesse's age, ran up and down the line of mules, checking harnesses, ropes and the trade goods, seeing that all was in readiness for the journey to the sea.

Jesse's heart sank. Where was Belshazzar?

And then the boy saw him. He saw the little white donkey coming toward him. The woman, her child in her arms, rode on his back while the man led him. The man from Nazareth had bought a new bridle for the donkey, too, and he had attached a foxtail to it as a talisman to keep Belshazzar's steps safe and steady. The donkey stepped daintily along, picking his way carefully across the cobblestones. His step was a sprightly one in spite of his burden of the woman and baby and the saddlebags on his back. When Jesse spied those he knew why the carpenter and his family were delayed and why he, Jesse, had got to the Joppa Gate first. The man had stopped in Jerusalem to buy supplies for the journey. Fleetingly the boy wondered about the gold, frankincense and myrrh he'd seen the three mad kings put before the baby in the stable in Bethlehem. Were those precious things in the saddlebags and in the other sack, the one the tall man in the brown robe carried over his shoulder?

Jesse stayed hidden in the darkness as the carpenter too spoke to the caravan leader. He watched the tall man give the greedy leader some coins. He saw the leader nod happily. So Belshazzar was to travel with the caravan too? Jesse looked on as the carpenter from Nazareth led the white donkey into the center of the procession of pilgrims and travelers.

The mute boy waited until the last of the band of travelers went through the inner of the two gates. Then he came out of the black shelter of the wall. Where Belshazzar went, Jesse ben Abdiel went. Even if the donkey did not want him, the boy meant to go. Belshazzar was in deadly danger while he traveled with the carpenter, his wife and baby. If Jesse had felt that Belshazzar would come willingly with him, Jesse would wait for his chance and steal him again. But he remembered all too well how the donkey had chosen the tall man in the brown robe.

At the very tail end of the caravan Jesse marched to the inner gate, but as he was about to pass the motionless guards, he heard a hoarse cry from behind him. The boy turned around to stare as a small, red-bearded, redhaired man in a black-and-gray striped robe came hurrying up on a fine brown mule, the finest mule with the most elaborate tasseled bridle the boy had ever seen—far finer than the one the carpenter had bought Belshazzar. Jesse saw the newcomer lean from the back of his mule to speak with the captain of King Herod's guards.

He seemed very excited. Jesse shrank back under the looming towers along the wall and sidled closer. He meant to hear what the man on the mule said, but the stranger spoke so quietly that Jesse could not catch one word.

But he heard the captain's loud reply easily enough. "Aye, a mule caravan left just now, sir. There were many people—pilgrims and other travelers. There was nothing unusual about the caravan except for some Arabian horses being taken to Rome to race in the Roman circus. There was no reason to stop the caravan, so I didn't."

The redhaired man's beard waggled as he bent even farther to speak to the black-cloaked captain.

"Aye, come to think on it," the soldier said after a pause, "there was an infant with them. As to whether it was a boy or a girl I can't say. I noticed because I became a father again not so long ago, myself. As for other children, I don't recall. . . ." He crooked his finger at another guard, who came at a run to his captain. "Did you see children traveling with that caravan bound for Joppa?" he asked the other soldier.

"Yes, there were children—pilgrims." The second guard's forehead wrinkled with thought under his helmet.

"Their ages?" demanded the red-bearded man eagerly, letting Jesse hear his squeaky voice for the first time.

"I am no judge of children's ages. They were all this high—or higher." He put his hand at his waist.

"Too old," muttered the man on the brown mule. "All too old—but for the baby."

"You didn't ask me if they were male or female children," put in the second guard.

"No matter—no matter!" The redhaired man was impatient to be away. He kicked his mule into a trot and left the gate to ride back into the city. But before he went, he stared into the darkness of the double gate, his expression a grim one, his eyes a bright light green in the torchlight. Never had Jesse ben Abdiel seen such eyes. They were like an animal's, not a man's. They reminded him of the luminous golden eyes of King Solomon, Nabal's old lion.

Jesse went through the double gate, thinking deeply. The Joppa Gate made a right-angle turn, so the two gates were not parallel to each other. That way each could be more easily protected, but the space between them was not a pleasant one. The air was dead and the walls loomed high and threatening on both sides of the boy. The single torch flickered low as if it were about to go out. The conversation of the guards and the very few words spoken by the stranger on the mule would not leave Jesse's mind. He thought, too, of the conversation of Caleb and Jonas, the men at the inn of the Damascus Gate. This was all the work of

Herod, Jesse knew. A spear of foreboding went
through the boy as he thought of the baby he had
seen at Bethlehem and again here in Jerusalem—
the baby marked for death.

But the baby did not really concern Jesse ben
Abdiel so much. It was a terrible thing that young
children were to be murdered, of course—but then
Herod had supposedly murdered his own children,
hadn't he? The baby meant little to Jesse. No one
human, except for Saul, cared for Jesse. Why should
Jesse care for anyone human now that his father
was dead? His uncle Habor had turned him out.
He, Jesse, was a dumb beast. He could only give
his best love to other mute creatures. The love he
gave Saul was a far lesser thing than his love for
the white donkey.

Jesse quickened his footsteps to pass through the
gloomy place between the walls. He'd seen the tall
carpenter three times now, and Jesse sensed something about him. The man was strong. Carpenters
had to be. He would fight if Herod's men tried to
kill his son. And if the carpenter fought, so would
Belshazzar. Once, months ago, one of the wrestlers
in Nabal's circus, not Reuben but the other one,
whose name Jesse could no longer remember, had
tried to beat Jesse for refusing to share some grapes
he'd stolen. Then the white donkey had shown the
stuff he was made of, lashing out with his hooves
so wildly that the big wrestler had fled. Yes, the

carpenter would put up a fight—and so would Belshazzar. Then they would all be slaughtered by the
swords of Herod's murderers. Perhaps somehow he,
Jesse, could save the white donkey he loved yet. . . .

Jesse hurried out through the outer gate into the
fresh-smelling night.

Once beyond the Joppa Gate, he began to run—
to catch up with the caravan on the road that led
to the sea.

VIII. THE BLACK CAMEL

The horse dealer was a desert nomad from Araby named Sokar.

Jesse had decided after a few moments of hurrying along the road that the nomad would be his best opportunity for traveling with the caravan that had swallowed up Belshazzar. He'd thought first that the leader could use another lad with a stick to beat the pack mules, but he'd soon discarded that idea. In the first place he didn't want to beat animals, and in the second place the caravan leader's boys had to run constantly up and down the line

129

of march, hitting a balky mule here and another slow one there. That was certainly no way to keep hidden from the carpenter's view, and the son of Abdiel meant to do just this. He'd keep a watchful eye on the white donkey while they traveled, but he wouldn't be spied out by Belshazzar or by the carpenter and his wife. Who knew if they'd found out before they left Bethlehem that a runaway boy from a shabby circus had stolen their donkey? The tag end of the procession was where Jesse meant to stay. That was also the place where the nomad traveled, to keep the dust made by his restless animals from the eyes of the travelers.

Before they camped for the night the boy had got into the good graces of the man from the desert. A filly broke loose from the side of her mother as the mare reared, frightened by a flash of lightning in the sky. The colt fled back toward Jerusalem as Sokar shouted and dashed on his horse after her, but it was Jesse who caught her by her neck rope. At a run the boy brought the beautiful milk-white filly to the nomad. The man grunted, bent and stroked her mane. In very poor Aramaic he spoke to Jesse. "Where do you go, boy?"

Jesse pointed to the west—in the direction of the sea.

"I go to Joppa, the seaport. I will pay you to help me with my horses. Speak up, boy. You will work for me?" Sokar spoke slowly, searching for his words in the unfamiliar speech of Israel.

Jesse went through his motions of showing that
he was a mute. After a time the nomad understood.
He grunted. "Well, no matter to me. You know what
I say, don't you? And *I* am master here."

Jesse nodded that he understood this.

Sokar nodded too. "Then it's agreed, boy. *I* give
the commands and *you* do as I say. Walk with the
mare, calm her down." The nomad gave his mount
his head and took his place beside the line of horses,
well pleased that he had a helper—and not at all
unpleased that he wouldn't have much conversation
with the boy in a language he found so difficult
to speak.

They stopped that night at a dirty little inn some
miles out of Jerusalem. Jesse knew how far they had
come. Traveling with Nabal's circus had taught him
to count the Roman mileposts along the way. He
knew they would move slowly—people afoot could
not travel rapidly over the poor roads of Israel,
roads that even the efficient Romans could not keep
in good repair.

Sokar tethered his horses in the open air, not far
from the wooden loggia that protected the poorer
travelers while the wealthier ones went inside to
sleep in the small rooms. After an evening meal of
thick dark wine, dates, flat bread and goat's-milk
cheese, supplied by the horse dealer, Jesse and Sokar
rolled up in their robes to sleep close to the white
horses, too valuable to be left unguarded for even
a moment. But before he slept, the nomad pulled

a very long sharp knife out of his robes and put it beside him. Jesse kept his eyes on the knife as he got up and moved to the other side of the snoring Sokar's fire, the side from which he could best see the carpenter and his family.

There they were, the man in brown sitting on the ground under the loggia, the woman and baby seated on some hay the innkeeper had put out for her and the other travelers. Behind them, as if he guarded them, stood Belshazzar. Jesse had often thought that, unlike other donkeys, Belshazzar had an expression to his face. Now he seemed to be dreaming as he watched the woman who held the infant. The inn door was half open behind them to let out the smoke from the cooking fires, and a light from somewhere inside bathed the little family and the donkey in a yellow glow. For a long time the boy watched them, long after the other travelers and pilgrims had gone to sleep. While he watched, he thought of many things, turning over the words of the men in the inn by the Damascus Gate and the questions of the green-eyed man in his mind. The son of Abdiel sighed, wondering what was going to happen to him and to Belshazzar. He could not truly permit himself to hope that he and the white donkey would be together again.

Late at night Jesse finally fell asleep, a nightmare-studded sleep filled with questioning strangers and long knives like Sokar's. He awoke when a chill dawn

breeze arose and blew across his face. Jesse realized
he was very thirsty. Sokar's fire burned low, and the
Arab slept on. Quietly, quietly as only a boy who
was an expert thief could move, the son of Abdiel
slipped away from his new master to the well in
the center of the inn courtyard. He stood on his
tiptoes first to see if he could see the carpenter still.
Yes, there he was—his long brown robe spread out
over him and over the feet of his wife. The white
blur behind them in the half-dark was Belshazzar,
sleeping. Jesse shook his head in wonder. Now why,
with all the gold they'd been given in Bethlehem by
the kings, did these people spend the night among
the poorest travelers? With Sokar it was different.
He feared robbers and wouldn't leave his horses for
a moment.

The boy drew water from the well, using the
dipper attached to it, and as he drank he looked
out over its rim toward the road they'd traveled.

His sharp ears caught the soft pad-padding sound
that only the feet of a camel made, and as Jesse
watched, a great black camel ridden by a man in a
dark robe went swiftly by under a lowering dawn-
streaked sky. The hooded rider stopped for a
moment, gazed sharply about him, and then when
he spied the boy watching him, hit the camel with
his whip. Jesse spilled water over his feet as he saw
the rider twist around in his saddle to look back at
the inn. A feeling of sudden uneasiness gripped the

mute boy. His sixth sense for trouble was working hard now. He'd had the warning premonition often in the hills above Arad while tending his uncle's sheep, and then all too often a slinking wolf or a bear had appeared out of the many ravines to try to snatch a lamb. He'd had it in Nabal's circus too, when there was going to be a fight between the circus folk and the villagers they'd cheated. Camels weren't too often seen on the roads of Israel, except in caravans. Men who rode black camels alone by night were even more rare.

Unseen by Sokar, Jesse made his way back to the fire and to the horses. When the nomad awoke, the boy was beside the white filly, combing her mane with his fingers, on the other side of the horses from the carpenter--a place where he could not be seen.

The morning meal was a handful of raisins and a barley cake, hastily eaten, because the caravan leader shouted that it was time for them to go. His boys ran with their sticks among the animals to get them to their feet. Now Jesse stepped in among Sokar's horses once more and peered under the belly of one to see how Belshazzar fared. He hoped the carpenter would protect the donkey from the lads with sticks. But there was no reason to worry. The white donkey was on his feet. Jesse watched closely while the carpenter watered and fed him. Belshazzar looked fine and fit, and the man from Nazareth hadn't put anything at all in his food or water that

Jesse had seen. The boy would swear to that. Yet when the man lifted his wife and son onto the donkey's back, Belshazzar moved out more sprightly than Jesse had ever seen him move. So the carpenter must have given the donkey something before they had left Jerusalem. That was the answer, of course. It was the only answer. There could be no other. Yesterday in Jerusalem, Belshazzar's strength had been ebbing swiftly.

As they went through Emmaus once more, the town where Jesse had joined Nabal's circus and had first seen the white donkey, Jesse kept an eye on Belshazzar. He had arranged it so he walked beside the Arabians, so that he could see the family from Nazareth, yet not be seen himself. The mute boy thought mournfully of Saul as they passed the inn of Gezer and trailed through the little town.

Jesse knew from overheard conversations of the caravan leader—which were not hard to hear because the leader always shouted—that the caravan would split at Zuph, some miles west of Emmaus. He knew from snatches of talk his ears had caught that most of the pilgrims came from Alexandria, in Egypt, where many, many thousands of Jews lived —where there were far more Jews than in Jerusalem. Yet these Egyptian Jews must come to the temple to worship too—even the Jews of Rome must come. That was the Law of Israel. The Alexandrians would go to Joppa—a Jewish port, he knew—to board ships for Egypt. Jesse ben Abdiel would not go to Joppa.

In Zuph, Sokar paid Jesse a few coins for his work with the horses when he learned the boy refused to go to Joppa with him. But the Arab could not understand why, if Jesse went to the sea also, he wouldn't go to Joppa.

Jesse remained in Zuph because of the carpenter. While the travelers and pilgrims took the road to Joppa, the carpenter and his family had remained by the well of Zuph. Jesse waited around the corner of a house to see what they did. Where Belshazzar went, he went, and Belshazzar did not go to Joppa. So, neither did Jesse! He did not know where he went, but he did not go to Joppa.

Sokar, the nomad from Araby, looked after the boy as he and his horses took the northern road and then shrugged his shoulders. What was an Israelite lad to him?

A few moments later the man in the brown robe lifted his wife and child onto the donkey's back and set out onto the southern road, the road to Ashkelon. Amazed, Jesse left his hiding place to stare after them. These people traveled *alone*—alone to a city of pagan Philistines. Why would they go to such a place when Joppa, a Jewish city, was closer? For a long, long moment the son of Abdiel did not know what to do, too surprised to think clearly. Then he knew. He would do as he had said he would— follow Belshazzar. He did not think beyond this decision.

A small ragged figure, the mute boy took the road that led south from Zuph as the mule caravan traveled out of the village on the north road.

Slowly the boy followed, trying to keep out of sight as much as he could but at the same time keeping Belshazzar and the donkey's new master in his view. It was not easy. There were few trees—only carob trees along this particular stretch of the road—and Jesse had to scurry from carob to carob to hide himself behind them. More than once he thought he saw the man in the brown robe looking back. More than once he thought that the man had spied him out, but then the carpenter turned about and went on his way again toward the Philistine city.

Jesse, son of Abdiel, his heart in his mouth, traveled past two milestones before it happened—before the tall man from Nazareth swung about for the fourth time and this time waved his arm. The gesture could not be mistaken. The boy had been seen. The man wanted him to come. Jesse hesitated in the middle of the road. There were no trees, no bushes and no ravines to hide him at that point on the way to Ashkelon. The sun came all at once from behind a dark cloud and beat down upon him, catching him up in the same wide shaft of violet radiance it gave to the family and the donkey.

Caught, Jesse ben Abdiel moved forward. He didn't want to go, but his feet seemed to move of their own accord, faster and faster, until he was running.

The woman bent her head over the baby. She took no notice of a panting Jesse in his soiled, tattered robe, but the carpenter spoke to him. "Do you too travel to Ashkelon, boy?"

Jesse glanced at the white donkey out of the corner of one eye. No, Belshazzar paid no more attention to him than the woman did. Jesse yearned to pat him, but didn't dare. Instead, he nodded in answer to the man's question. Yes, he too went to the city of the Philistines.

"Well, then, come along with us," said the man from Nazareth in a kindly tone. "We have food and water enough. Tell me, what is your name?"

They wanted him! The boy stared, astounded, until the carpenter repeated his question. Jesse put his hand to his mouth, shook his head, and, stooping, wrote in the mud of the road, "Jesse."

"Ah," the carpenter murmured. "Jesse is a name of honor in Israel. I am sorry that you cannot speak, but come with us now."

Out of the reach of King Herod, thought the boy, his brain almost exploding with the lightning-swift thought! Belshazzar would be safe in Ashkelon. Herod's hand would not reach to Ashkelon. The city of Philistines, for all that it was a heathen city, was the safest place to go. Jesse nodded again and again as the carpenter led the donkey along the road.

With the little family the mute boy traveled throughout the rest of that short day. His gaze was on the white donkey as often as he dared without making the man suspicious. How Jesse yearned to touch and embrace Belshazzar, who ignored him! Dark night came down as swiftly as the stranger's tall camel could run, and at twilight the carpenter led Belshazzar to another inn, one even smaller and humbler than the first. This time it rained very hard, and the carpenter took a room for his wife and son and put Belshazzar in the inn stable. By gestures Jesse let him know that he would sleep in the stable loft and watch over the donkey. The carpenter nodded and had simple food, the sort of food Jesse guessed the man and his wife were eating themselves, sent out to the grateful boy where he sat beside the donkey. Finally, after long caressing an indifferent Belshazzar, a mournful boy climbed up to the loft to roll up in his old robe in the scented hay. How cold, how very cold it was. His teeth chattered, and as full dark came and the desert winds blowing from the east toward the sea grew even more chill, the boy moved away, in spite of himself, from the loft opening. He'd wanted to watch the inn. His curiosity about the family from Nazareth gave him no rest—the family that had wanted him to travel with them. He'd marked out the tiny window of the inn room where the man from Nazareth rested for the night, and he'd hoped to keep the star-point of the carpenter's oil lamp in his gaze, but he could not. The wind came too icy through the loft opening for him to keep his vigil. Jesse rose to his knees, trying to close one side of the wooden shutter, and then in the dead moonlight that had followed the rain, he saw it again—the camel, motionless, atop a hill to the east, its rider looking down at the inn in the hollow.

Jesse ben Abdiel made a low sound of fear in his throat. Last night he had been upset and uneasy. Now he was frightened—truly frightened. Why hadn't the rider reached his destination, wherever that might be? Israel was not a very large land, and the mysterious rider traveled by night as well as probably by day. A camel could move far more swiftly than a man or a donkey could walk. The idea that he was seeing a second rider and a second similar camel did not enter Jesse's mind. He knew it was the same hooded man and the same black camel.

IX. THE DAUGHTER
OF MARCUS TULLIUS

During the night Jesse dreamed. First of all he saw
flashing lights and wheeling stars in a deep-blue sky.
Then he heard a sound as of a great bell being struck,
a sound that vibrated through his entire body. And
then he saw a picture in his dream—the picture of
a caravan, a large caravan made up of many men
and many animals.

When he woke up Jesse ben Abdiel felt rested
and refreshed, although he knew he had slept little

because of the cold. He was refreshed because he now believed he knew the answer to his fears about the man on the black camel. The boy feared the unknown rider chiefly because he, Belshazzar, and the family from Nazareth were now alone. His dream picture had shown him the way, the safest way: to travel with a large caravan. They needed to join another caravan. When they had been with a caravan they had been safe, although Jesse had not believed it at the time. He had been wrong and knew it now. Jesse hoped that one would come along, and that they would join it before they had gone far on the road to Ashkelon the next day.

Not long after dawn the carpenter was up and about and came to the stable to see how the donkey and the boy fared. The man carried grain for the animal and a bowl of lentil porridge for Jesse. The boy ate swiftly, never taking his eyes from the donkey and the man, but he saw nothing being taken from the man's purse or robe and dropped into the water or grain. Enviously Jesse looked on as Belshazzar rubbed his head on the man's arm. What could it be, the boy asked himself, that makes Belshazzar love this man? The carpenter did not pamper the old donkey as Jesse had always done. He seemed to think of him only as a beast of burden, but otherwise treated him very well.

Soon after, they went slowly along the way to Ashkelon, Jesse walking behind the man and the donkey. Now the boy was a little more accustomed to the family from Nazareth, although he was still embarrassed and wary around them. He stole glances at the woman and baby now and then and after a time decided that she was truly beautiful. Her eyes were somewhat bluer than those of the Galileans of the circus, and her hair was a soft russet-brown. The baby, too, was beautiful, with a crown of yellowish curls and eyes the exact color of his mother's, but there was something to Jesse's mind even more remarkable about the carpenter's son than his beauty. The baby had never once cried. What kind of infant was that? In Arad babies did nothing but fret and wail and get in the way of their parents, demanding care and attention.

So Jesse walked on, and as he walked, a strange feeling of peace came over him. In spite of the nagging at the back of his mind because of the black camel and because of Belshazzar's age and illness, Jesse felt a still calmness. He was almost lulled into a sense of safety. The black camel was now nowhere to be seen on the sunlit road that led to the sea. The sun was so hot on the boy's back that he wished he could take off his robe and warm himself. The puddles in the road from the rain of the evening were drying swiftly, but Belshazzar stepped over them, now lifting his hooves higher than Jesse had ever seen him. The donkey certainly had a spring in his gait. Once more the boy wondered what the carpenter put into the donkey's food and when he did it. Perhaps Belshazzar didn't receive his tonic every single day. It could be a long-lasting potion the man in the brown robe gave him. Medicine that had an effect for days could explain the donkey's long-lasting health when the boy had stolen him in Bethlehem, too.

Jesse made up his mind about something as they passed the third milestone of the day's journey. He knew that the carpenter would stop before long to rest beside the road. Then Jesse would try to communicate with him and show him that he wanted to travel with a caravan. Perhaps he would even show the man that they were followed by a man on a camel, although how he was to do that by pictures drawn in the dirt of the road Jesse didn't quite know. But all the same he meant to try.

When they reached the next milestone, the carpenter helped the woman down to give Belshazzar a rest. Jesse squatted before the man and began to draw the first figures—himself and the three from Nazareth and the donkey.

Then, before he could go on, Jesse heard it—the sound from behind them, the sound of many feet. He listened only for a moment and quickly jumped to his feet, alarmed. He knew what terrible thing it was—no caravan from Jerusalem headed for Ashkelon, no, indeed! No caravan at all! It was the earthshakers coming—Romans—Roman soldiers —dozens of them.

In a flash Jesse ben Abdiel had fled from the side of the road to hide himself behind a boulder. There he cowered while the Romans came steadily on, the stamp of their marching feet growing ever louder. But as the boom of their footsteps came closer, another sound, a beautiful one, like a birdsong, rose high, piercing the *boom boom*. Jesse knew many of the birds of Israel, but he had never heard one sing so sweetly as this one.

The boy peered out from behind his rock to see what was happening, and what he saw astounded him. Jesse had deserted the carpenter, his wife, the child and even Belshazzar in his panic-stricken terror of the Romans, but he had believed that they would run away to hide too. They hadn't! How foolhardy of them. The man stood calmly, leaning on his staff, looking eastward in the direction from which the Romans came. As the white donkey gazed at her the woman sat quietly on the milestone singing to her baby. It was her voice, not a birdsong at all, that Jesse ben Abdiel heard. While the terrible Roman conquerors of Israel marched down upon her, the carpenter's wife sat by the road and *sang!*

Jesse was astonished. He grew even more astonished as the Roman legionaries drew abreast of them. The family from Nazareth did not move as the officer, his red horsehair helmet crest and red cloak aflame in the sunlight and his bronze breastplate as bright as any copper mirror, passed them on a fine bay horse. They did not move while the first group of soldiers swung by, their faces set under their helmets, their weapons at their belts and their other gear over their backs. Their short swords, the famous terrible short swords of Rome, gleamed dully, as did their shields. Their heavy sandals were hobnailed, and they churned the puddle-filled road into a mass of flaking mud as they swept by.

The two white mules, who carried the fine-curtained litter, a litter of gilded wood and leather, picked their way through the mire. They were followed by the gray mule of the veiled woman, who rode close beside the litter. More soldiers followed her gray mule, soldiers who looked neither to the right nor to the left and who did not seem to see the little family from Nazareth clustered around the milestone.

Finally the Romans and their supply carts had passed. The sound of their sandals began to fade away. The boy heard the woman's voice continuing her song, and then he heard the sound of hooves. The woman who rode the gray mule came cantering back to the carpenter and his wife. Jesse saw her lean from her mule, her red veil still over her face, to talk with the family from Nazareth. He could not hear her words, but as she began to speak, the carpenter's wife stopped singing. The veiled woman seemed to be asking swift questions, and she did not speak long with the tall man. But when she had finished, the carpenter lifted his wife onto

Belshazzar's back and took the donkey's bridle in his hand to follow the veiled newcomer. The family from Nazareth was going to *join the Romans!*

The boy's wits raced. He bolted out of his hiding place to dash along the road toward the donkey and the carpenter. When the tall man in the brown robe looked behind him and raised his arm and beckoned to him, the boy darted toward him. Where Belshazzar went, Jesse ben Abdiel went, and Belshazzar now traveled with the Romans, the rulers of the whole world. Jesse trusted the man from Nazareth, a carpenter like his father. Where would the donkey be safer? Where would the family be safer than with the awful Romans, as long as the donkey behaved himself, not braying or biting or kicking, and as long as he could keep up with the marchers? The rider of the black camel would not worry him now, the boy knew. As for Jesse himself, he planned to step warily among the mystifying, terrible Romans. The woman with the red veil had not invited Jesse to travel with the soldiers.

At midday the Roman columns halted to eat a handful of grain and to drink their sour red wine. Then the veiled woman came back once more, this time on foot, to the Israelites, who traveled with the legionaries behind the supply carts.

She removed her veil now, so Jesse saw her face. The woman was small-boned and thin, her skin an olive color and her large eyes a deep brown. "I am Saphir, the daughter of Mordecai," she told the carpenter and his wife. "I am a slave to Marcus Tullius, the Roman governor of Egypt, and have been for three years now, but I was born in Judea —in Beersheba."

That, of course, explained the woman's Jewish name and her fine Aramaic, Jesse decided. The fact that she was a Roman slave explained the handsome mule and her fine clothing. Her red robe was edged with silver embroidery of pomegranates and grapes.

Saphir went on, "My mistress, Tullia, is a little girl—only seven years old. She was ill, very ill of a fever she took in Alexandria. We came months past to Israel to consult the Greek doctors by the Sea of Galilee. Tullia is better, I think, and stronger because of Galilee's dry climate, but she is very bored riding all day in her litter. She says that she saw the countryside of Israel when she came from Egypt and has no wish to see it again, so she keeps the litter curtains drawn. She loves music. It was Tullia who heard you first singing by the side of the road and knew that it was a human voice before we came abreast of you. I heard you too, of course, and thought I listened to a birdsong. As I told you before, my mistress asks that you travel with us to Ashkelon, where we take ship to Egypt, and to sing for her when she sends for you." Saphir's curious but gentle eyes were on Jesse's face now. "Whose boy is this? I do not think he, too, is your son."

"He is Jesse," replied the carpenter simply. "He cannot speak. The boy is a mute."

"Is he, then?" the slave woman asked. Her voice was kind. "Do you go to Ashkelon also, Jesse?"

Jesse ben Abdiel nodded. He began to sketch in the dust figures of a few sheep and of a small shepherd with his staff. Finally he rubbed out the drawing of the staff and instead put pipes to the shepherd's mouth. For some reason he did not understand or question, Saphir's words about music had interested him, and when he finished the drawing he pulled his shepherd's pipes out of the bosom of his robe, the pipes he had not played since he left Arad.

Saphir clasped her hands at the sight of the pipes. "How wonderful!" the slave exclaimed. "Can you play them well?"

Jesse nodded. In Arad a few people had said he could play them very, very well—his only talent. He put them up to his lips and played as merry a tune as he could remember, one he'd sometimes heard in his mind but never played during his contented moments with Saul.

"That was very fine," commented Saphir. "Perhaps you will come up to the litter and play to amuse my mistress as we go along? Can you keep pace with the soldiers?"

Jesse nodded but rolled his eyes toward the Romans, who sat as they ate with their backs to him and the family from Nazareth.

The woman spoke soothingly. "Do not fear the legionaries, Jesse. They will not harm you. The officer who takes us to Ashkelon is under the command of Marcus Tullius. He will protect all of you because Tullia wishes it. The officer knows how much his master in Egypt loves his daughter. Marcus Tullius, who has lost his wife in a shipwreck and who has no other children, gives his daughter whatever she asks. . . ." Saphir sighed, reaching out to touch the baby's face. "It has not been easy for my little mistress living alone in that great marble palace in cold, windswept Alexandria." She changed the subject quickly. "What a beautiful child you have!" she said of the carpenter's baby. "Is he a good child? Does he cry much?"

The carpenter's wife shook her head, then opened her blue cloak so Saphir could admire her son's fingers as well as his face, and the slave woman sighed once more. Jesse also leaned forward now to see the baby more closely. The child's face shone in the sunlight, and his hair was a tangled halo of gold.

"I must serve Marcus Tullius for another three years," said Saphir. "My father was forced to sell me into slavery to pay his debts when his harvest failed, but, as you know, a Jewish slave serves but six years to a Roman master. I wish to return to Beersheba and marry and have children of my own, but how can I leave Tullia when I've come to love her as my own?"

Jesse gasped at this. Who could love a Roman? Was Saphir a madwoman in spite of her gentle words?

Saphir understood the boy's gasp. She smiled at him. "Tullia is not like the others, Jesse, although she is a Roman. She has been sad since her mother died. I am afraid that she returns to Alexandria too soon for her health, but Marcus Tullius has sent for her."

Now the slave woman put up her veil again. "I will tell my mistress about you, Jesse, and your shepherd's pipes. If I send someone to you when we begin to march, come at once to play."

In a flutter of perfumed robes Saphir was gone toward the head of the procession, where the curtained litter and her gray mule waited, guarded by legionaries.

After Jesse had shared some of the carpenter's cheese and bread and drunk from the gourd he'd filled the night before at the inn well, they were on their way once more. The ground trembled under the nailed sandals of Rome. For a while Jesse practiced playing his pipes, but then gave it up. It did not seem that the Roman girl wanted him after all. But in the late afternoon a legionary came running up to the boy—a tall, thickset, reddish-blond man, a Gaul, a man from a land far to the west, a land also ruled by Rome. He spoke no word but only pointed to Jesse and then jerked his thumb back toward the litter. He didn't wait for the boy to join him but hurried back to his place at the head of the line behind Tullia's mules.

Jesse took a deep breath, caught the carpenter's eye and grinned as much of a grin as he could muster up. The carpenter nodded as the boy hesitated for another moment, looking at Belshazzar. Jesse guessed he could safely leave the donkey in the man's care. But walking ahead of the people from Nazareth, how could he see if the man gave Belshazzar a tonic? Jesse ben Abdiel shrugged. That could not be helped now. He took to his heels, running alongside the road, overtaking the Romans, but at the same time keeping as far from them as he could.

He did not see Tullia. The curtains on his side of the litter were never opened as he played, but on the other side, where Saphir rode, they were. "Play a tune the sheep of Israel dance to, Jesse," the woman called to him once. "I have told my mistress how the sheep dance in Judea, but she will not believe that they can. She says sheep do not dance." So Jesse played one of his more sprightly tunes to please the Roman girl, and then he played many others, tunes he'd heard in his head, tunes he made up. Finally Saphir asked for a song she knew, a song that women in Arad sometimes crooned to their babies. Jesse knew it, of course, and played it too.

Then Saphir put her finger to her lips and motioned for him to walk over to her. The curtains were now drawn on her side of the litter. "She sleeps. Tullia sleeps." Saphir put a silver shekel, a whole shekel, into Jesse's hand. So much money for only playing his shepherd's pipes!

"You've done well, Jesse," she told him. "Play your pipes often—play those tunes I've never heard before in Israel and you'll never go hungry. How many melodies you know! It is remarkable. Now, go back to your friends from Nazareth. Tullia wishes the carpenter's wife to sing for her tonight after the evening meal."

Jesse scooted off the road, not to be trampled by the oncoming Romans and their carts, and stood, panting, as they swung and creaked by him. It was near sunset and he hoped they would camp for the night soon. He was tired. The Romans set a good pace, although not as fast a pace as he'd seen them on their march to the Dead Sea months past. Their slower pace was probably out of consideration for Tullia, to keep her from being jostled in her litter. But keeping up with the legionaries and playing his pipes at the same time had badly winded the boy.

He stood waiting while the family from Nazareth came up to him. Belshazzar had kept pace with the Romans wonderfully well. Jesse marveled at him, remembering the dark days on the road to Bethlehem when the white donkey's strength ebbed away with every step he took.

That night the soldiers made their usual camp.

They dug a ditch around it for better protection, and they set a guard about it so no one could enter it without the permission of their officer. The legionaries paid no attention to the ragged Jewish boy or to the old white donkey the boy lay down beside, while the carpenter and his wife and child went to the tent that had been put up for the Roman girl and her slave woman. Some few of them stopped to listen as they prepared their night's food when the woman's pure voice rose in song. They spoke to one another in their various languages, the tongues of Gaul, Germany, Spain, Greece and Dalmatia, and sometimes even in Latin, the language of Rome. As the men of Israel did not enter the armies of Rome, not one word was said in Aramaic. Jesse ben Abdiel could not eavesdrop here, much as he would have liked to learn the news from Jerusalem. As the boy stroked the white donkey's ears, his thoughts grew dark.

What of King Herod? Had he begun to murder the tiny boys of Israel already? The man at the inn of the Damascus Gate had said that the soldiers of Herod would begin to kill the innocent children in three days. That would mean that Herod had begun the slaughter this very day. The mute boy's thoughts went now to the carpenter's baby. Surely that baby, at least, was safe? Ashkelon was not a Jewish city. Herod's soldiers had no power in the city of the Philistines. And by traveling with Romans, no matter where they marched, the carpenter had put his son out of any kind of danger.

Lulled by his thoughts about safety in Ashkelon and by the presence of dozens of Roman soldiers surrounding him, the tired boy fell asleep, his head pillowed on Belshazzar's side as in the old days.

Jesse ben Abdiel did not see the tall black camel race by that night. He did not see the rider's eyes range over the campfires to spy out the white donkey and the boy, nor did he know how the man pricked up his ears when he heard the voice of the woman singing a lullaby in the scarlet tent. The son of Abdiel did not hear a shouted challenge from the Roman guards, because there was none and no reason for one. The black camel did not break its stride as it sped westward on the way to Ashkelon, and it did not approach the entrance to the Roman camp. A traveler who minded his own affairs, even if he traveled by the dead of night, was of no concern to Rome.

X. THE CITY OF DOVES

The next morning Jesse and the carpenter's family got underway early, as soon as the Romans could eat and break camp. The boy knew from Saphir's words as she mounted her donkey that they would reach Ashkelon by dusk. His heart sank at her words, even though he knew that at Ashkelon, Belshazzar and the baby would surely be safe from Herod's men.

But what would happen there? Would the carpenter go on to Alexandria, to Egypt, with the Roman girl? That was what little Tullia had asked

156

Saphir to ask the family from Nazareth last night.
But the invitation had not included Jesse ben Abdiel,
whose shepherd's pipes had not pleased the girl as
much as the woman's singing had. Saphir had shaken
her head at the question in the boy's eyes. No, he
had not been invited. Jesse sighed as he brought up
the rear behind the carts, behind the little family
he'd first seen in Bethlehem. If they went to Egypt,
they'd probably take Belshazzar, their donkey, with
them. Jesse knew that he would never see the donkey
again if that happened. He could not afford to go
to Egypt—not with one shekel and four leptons, all
he had. Jesse kept on sighing. But he was going to
be with Belshazzar as long as he possibly could,
even though the donkey now paid no heed to his
former master at all. Belshazzar was affectionate
with the carpenter, who had not yet said they traveled to Egypt. Enviously the mute boy had noticed,
too, how the donkey never took his eyes from the
woman and child. The moment she dismounted,
he turned his head toward her and seemed to gaze
directly at her and her baby. The night before, Belshazzar had even rested with his head toward the
scarlet tent, and Jesse had awakened late to find
the animal standing near the woman and the sleeping child as if he guarded them. Oh, thought Jesse
ben Abdiel, how I wish I could ask the carpenter
what he gives Belshazzar before he takes him away
from me forever. The carpenter, a good and gentle

man, would tell him this great secret, the boy felt certain, but how could he ask such a question by only drawing pictures? How could he make the man from Nazareth understand?

While Jesse was pondering this question, he heard another sound besides the tramp of soldier's heavy sandals—not the sound of human feet but of hooves. An animal came swiftly along the road to Ashkelon. The boy turned at once to see and in the distance spied a cloud of dust, a cloud just big enough to mean a single rider. The thought of the black camel came to the boy, but he dismissed it at once. This was not the shuffle of any camel but the hard ring of horse's hooves. Almost immediately a scarlet-cloaked rider on a gray horse broke out of the dust. It was another Roman, an officer, judging from the red horsehair plume in his helmet, and the horse on closer inspection was a black one, not gray at all. It had been ridden hard—so hard that it was lathered whitish.

The Roman courier shouted when he saw the column of legionaries, and the officer who was taking Tullia to her father in Egypt galloped back along the column to meet the newcomer. Behind him cantered Saphir on her mule, sent by her mistress to know who rode so swiftly to the seaport.

Tullia's officer hailed the courier as Galba, a Roman name Jesse had once heard used in Jerusalem when some Israelites were speaking of a particularly hated pagan soldier of the Roman garrison.

Galba spoke in Latin to the other legionary, his
voice sharp and loud. He didn't speak long, but his
face was dark with anger, and Jesse heard the word
"Herod" again and again in the Roman's words.
Tullia's officer's face, too, grew more stern by the
moment as he listened, his eyes narrowing with rage.
Then the two men shook their heads as if they agreed
about something evil, clasped one another's forearms
with their right hands, and Galba, digging his heels
into the black's lather-circled sides, was off on his
way, leaving the column in his biting, choking cloud
of yellow dust.

Saphir had gone pale as she listened. When Galba
had gone, she put her hands to her face. She swayed
on her mule as the man from Nazareth caught at
its reins. The slave woman looked down at him, her
eyes brimming with tears. "The Roman courier
brought news from Jerusalem. King Herod believes
that the true Messiah has been born in Israel. Yesterday his soldiers murdered every boy child in the
land under the age of two years. Herod thinks a
child who was born in Israel will take his throne
from him."

Jesse bowed his head in grief, although the news
was no surprise to him, while the carpenter's wife
drew her blue mantle over her head as Saphir went
on weeping. "The courier, Galba, has exhausted
three post horses since he left the city of Herod

yester eve. He takes the evil news to Rome—a journey of fifty-four days. Even the *Romans* in Jerusalem
are angry! Did you see how angry Galba was?"

"It is a terrible thing," the carpenter told her. He
was calm but his eyes were very sad.

"Galba accused King Herod openly of this hideous
crime. He hopes Herod will be punished by the
Romans. Our Roman officer will inform Marcus
Tullius in Egypt of the insult to Roman power."

The slave woman rode closer to the carpenter as
the dust cloud blew away. "Do not fear for your
son," she told him and the woman. "I can guess
what you must be thinking now, but you are safe
with us—with Romans. Come to Egypt with us. Your
baby will be safe there."

"We shall come," replied the man from Nazareth
simply. "We shall go to Egypt."

Jesse's eyes filled with tears like Saphir's. The
carpenter's decision had sealed the donkey's fate.
Now the mute boy would surely lose his donkey forever. But strangely, he didn't think so much of that
any more. He had become almost resigned to Belshazzar's loss. Now that he had heard the terrible
news, he was suddenly terrified for the beautiful
baby. The memory of the black camel and the sin-
ister searching rider plucked at him and made him
make up his mind. He would communicate with the
people from Nazareth about the camel somehow.

He caught Saphir's eyes to plead with her to give

him her attention, but she turned sadly away, saying, "I must tell my mistress the news Galba takes to Rome. It will grieve her." And she rode away.

Jesse pulled at the carpenter's sleeve, and the man looked at the boy. Jesse made his finger gesture that meant a four-legged animal. Then he stooped and swiftly drew the figure of a camel and a rider. Finally he pointed behind him, gesturing violently.

The man from Nazareth put his work-callused hand on the boy's shoulder. "Yes, lad, I know. My wife and I, we know. All will be well!"

The carpenter, too, turned away from the mute boy to go to Belshazzar, who had halted, waiting to be led farther along the way to Ashkelon. Jesse took up his pipes, and as he walked along, he played a plaintive, unhappy melody, the saddest one he knew. In his music he could give way to his misery and concern, even though no one could understand it when he tried to show it in other ways.

At dusk the soldiers of Marcus Tullius reached their destination, Ashkelon, the city of the heathen Philistines. As they entered the tall bronze gates in the city wall, Jesse ben Abdiel looked about with deep curiosity. He had heard a few things of Ashkelon while he traveled with Nabal's circus. The boy had heard Nabal and the fortuneteller speak of this city with horror and disgust. The ropedancer, who hailed from the Philistine city, wisely never spoke of his birthplace, valuing his safety among the other performers. Philistines were unpopular folk.

The Eternal was not worshiped in Ashkelon. The people of this city were not Jewish. Many of them had come from the islands out in the dark sea, and others from the north along the Syrian coast. They had brought their goddess with them, a goddess whose sacred animal was the dove. There were hundreds of thousands of white doves everywhere in Ashkelon. They bedeviled Jesse, who flung his arms about wildly to get rid of them. They lit on Belshazzar's back and on his neck and even tried to sit on his tail as he swished it about angrily, trying to get rid of the pesky birds.

The carpenter also attempted for a time to shoo the doves off, but it was hopeless. Of course the Romans weren't bothered. Romans refused to believe they could ever look ridiculous. Not even when the doves perched on their shoulders and the tops of their helmets and tried to peck at their shiny helmet earflaps did the soldiers move to brush them away. But for Belshazzar, Jesse noticed, the birds were horrible. The old donkey had to step gingerly to keep from treading on them as he followed the Roman carts, and more than once a cloud of white feathers drifted into the air as a dove squawked in rage and flapped away, his tail caught under a donkey hoof.

Ashkelon was very different from all other cities and villages the boy had seen. It lay on a hill in a half circle around a bay. This day the Mediterranean Sea was no clear bright blue. Jesse was frightened when he looked upon it for the first time. It was so very large and so very wide. The Mediterranean was dark, as dark as the wine of Israel, while the sky above it was gray. The north winds blowing down from Syria were very cold. The people of Ashkelon were different too. They weren't at all like the people Jesse had known in Israel. They wore much heavier clothing, robes and gowns of brightly colored wool, and Jesse noticed how they glared at the hated Roman conquerors with their light-colored eyes. Most of the people Jesse had known in his native land had brown eyes or, rarely, blue-green eyes, while many men and women of Ashkelon had blue eyes. But there were other differences too, he decided. All the people in the city of doves uncovered their hair in public, making Jesse marvel. The woman of Ashkelon brazenly bound up their brown hair with gay ribbon bands. Jewish women modestly kept their hair covered, as Saphir and the carpenter's wife did. Jesse noticed, though, how well the donkeys were treated in Ashkelon. They had fine white saddlecloths with red designs on them, saddlecloths that appealed to the boy. Jesse had long wished for a nice saddlecloth for Belshazzar, but he had never seen one that he could safely steal.

Jesse and the others clattered over the cobbles of the city following the Romans. He had no idea where he went. That was up to the officer who led them. To take his mind off his troubles, the boy looked about him. What he could spy of the buildings of Ashkelon through the wheeling flocks of white birds made him start in surprise. How much wood the people of Ashkelon used! Wood was very precious in Israel, and he heard the carpenter, a true craftsman, catch his breath excitedly as he too noticed.

Then they turned a sharp corner and found themselves before a very high red brick wall. At a command from their officer, the legionaries crashed to a halt, and the gates were flung open by more Roman soldiers. Jesse craned his neck to look around the back of a supply cart. He began to worry again. Would they be allowed to stay inside those heavy wood Roman gates? They looked safe enough to him, but his sixth sense was working hard once more. He sensed danger, but from whom and what he did not know. He looked about him, but he saw nothing threatening—nothing worse than the doves. He and the family from Nazareth waited while Tullia in her litter was taken inside the gates. Jesse kept his eyes on them, worrying.

But Saphir soon ended that for him by hurrying back to them. "This is the Roman garrison," she announced. "It is the only house in the city where the Lady Tullia would be permitted to stay, of

course, for it is the house of the most important
Roman, an old friend of Tullia's father's. My little
mistress has not forgotten you. She says all of you
are to stay here in the servants' quarters with me.
I am sorry, but it is the best I can do to keep you
safe. You'll have to sleep near slaves, but I have a
chamber set aside for you. You will have some rest."
She nodded at the baby. "You will hear no wailing
and grieving for little boy children here in Ashkelon,
a city Herod does not rule. All Israelites who come
here will find refuge. Herod's arm can never reach
so far from Jerusalem, the Eternal be praised.

"Come with me," Saphir went on. "Tomorrow at
dawn we'll take a ship for Alexandria."

Jesse hesitated until the tall carpenter tapped him
on the shoulder. Then, obediently, he and Belshazzar went forward into the Roman garrison, the gates
slamming shut behind them, nearly catching Belshazzar's switching tail as he shook off yet one more
dove.

The man in the brown robe lifted his wife and
child from Belshazzar's back. Of course, Belshazzar
could not go into a Roman house, although sometimes the poorer people in Israel kept animals on
the ground floor of their houses. Jesse wasn't pleased
and shook his head when a slave came and tried
to take Belshazzar off to the Roman stables, and
Saphir told the slave sharply to leave the donkey
alone. The boy wanted to be with Belshazzar. He

would stay outside the house with the animal. As they walked by, the thin nervous greyhounds the Romans kept as hunting dogs dashed out into the courtyard to snap at the donkey's heels. Jesse saw Belshazzar look at them out of the corner of one eye. The dogs fell back, barking wildly, until a slave called them off.

The family from Nazareth and the boy and the white donkey followed Saphir to a small plain door at the side of the house, where they were met by a very tall slave, a woman with golden-yellow hair worn in thick braids to her waist. She eyed the couple for a moment, then shook her head. But Saphir spoke to her and the woman shut the door.

"The German slave will prepare the chamber for you and when it is ready will come for us. My mistress is in good hands in this house. I will go to her in a moment."

Saphir sat on the marble slab that was the doorstep. Jesse stood beside the white donkey and watched while the carpenter's wife seated herself beside the slave woman and opened the baby's robe to let him kick and play awhile. Saphir took the child's foot in her hand, bent her head, and kissed it. "You've come far," Jesse heard Saphir say. "Your poor donkey must be very weary. Romans walk so swiftly. They are always in a hurry." The slave looked up at the carpenter, who stood beside Jesse. "Let me hear once more of your wonderful dream in Israel, Joseph."

"I saw the shining one, the angel, and heard his words, telling me that I should take my wife and child and go down into Egypt. That is why we go with you to Alexandria."

While the man spoke the baby laughed and reached out toward the donkey, who moved forward and lowered his head so the child could grab at the foxtail in his bridle. Jesse was astonished. Belshazzar had never done such a thing before. The carpenter's child grabbed wildly again and again but could not quite catch the foxtail.

"Oh, what a remarkable child he is!" Saphir exclaimed. "What other child so young would grasp for things? He sees everything. I almost believe he understands what we say. This is no common baby—that I know! I sometimes think he is more than I—"

But her words were cut off by the sudden appearance of the yellow-haired woman, who beckoned to her fellow slave. The carpenter's wife went with the German and Saphir into the house, but the tall man from Nazareth stayed behind with Jesse and the donkey.

"Come, Jesse," he said to the boy.

Jesse ben Abdiel drew back and shook his head. He'd made up his mind. He pointed at the donkey. No, he would stay in the brick-walled courtyard with the animal. If the carpenter was with the child, Jesse thought he would be safe.

"Do as you please, lad, but the nights are chill and

wet here by the sea. You'll have food brought to you, I'm sure. Are you hungry?"

Jesse shook his head again and opened his hands, then touched his old cloak. Yes, he knew it grew cold, but his cloak and his father's, folded over his shoulder as always, gave warmth enough. Yes, he was hungry. He nodded to show that.

The carpenter too went into the Roman house, leaving Jesse on the doorstep, thinking, watching Belshazzar. Here was his perfect chance, the boy told himself, to steal the white donkey for the second time. But he decided against it again. He couldn't steal from people who had befriended him and who had wanted him to travel with them. Anyway, the donkey preferred them. And Jesse remembered how Belshazzar's health had gradually failed when he was away from the man from Nazareth.

A man slave brought water and grain to Belshazzar and then the golden-haired woman carried a platter of food to Jesse, roast meats and fine bread, such as he'd never known existed. He had never tasted such wonderful things before, but he had little appetite for them. He left his food half eaten and sat with his head in his hands while the donkey stood patiently in front of him, waiting, his eyes on the door the carpenter and his family had gone through.

Jesse ben Abdiel leaned against the side of the commander's door as the white mists of the sea curled over the high walls on long questing fingers into the courtyard of the Roman garrison of Ashkelon. He pulled his cloak and his father's about him, thankful that the doves had flown away, and after a time his head began to nod, but he would not go to sleep. He yawned and sat up straight. This was his last night with Belshazzar. So, he would not sleep *it* away.

For a little while the white donkey remained beside his former master. Belshazzar had eaten all the grain the slave had brought him, but he was still hungry. His appetite had grown by leaps and bounds since the carpenter had found him in Jerusalem again. The donkey glanced about him, took a long final look at the door shut tight against him, and walked daintily through the mists toward a cart of hay pulled up not far from the slave quarters, waiting for the stable slaves to fork the hay into the mangers of the Roman horses and mules. There were tempting long wisps sticking out of the side of the cart, and no one was about in the courtyard to catch a small white battle-scarred donkey from Israel stealing a little hay.

Jesse saw all of this, and in spite of his unhappiness he had to grin. Now, this *was* like the donkey he'd once known. Well, the rich Romans could afford to lose a little hay. Jesse noticed how quietly Belshazzar moved now. The boy knew the donkey had been badly beaten more than once by the per-

formers in Nabal's circus and by Nabal himself for
stealing fodder before Jesse joined the circus. Belshazzar, too, could hear the soldiers who had escorted the Roman girl shouting and laughing and
calling to each other in their barracks. There were
also sounds from the commander's house, murmurs
of slaves in the kitchens and the barking of the
greyhounds. The boy laughed as he saw the donkey
cock a wary ear toward the nearest and most dangerous sounds. The white donkey would be careful.

Clever Belshazzar made it to the cart unnoticed.
No one saw him but Jesse, who rose slowly to his
feet, worried now about the sentries, the two Roman
legionaries who stood one on each side of the heavily
barred gate. Jesse doubted if they would care if a
donkey stole a little hay. Roman soldiers were above
that sort of thing. Beside that fact, Jesse could
scarcely make them out in the mists. He hoped that
meant they could not see him or the donkey either.

Jesse could tell that Belshazzar thought the hay
was excellent by the happy way he chewed. The
little donkey finished the wisps quickly, and still no
one was looking, except Jesse, who hadn't beaten
him off. So the donkey moved around to the back
of the cart, where the golden hay stuck out in even
finer toothsome tufts. He reached forward with his
teeth and tugged out a good biteful. Belshazzar ate
it and reached, then, for the third huge bite.

This time, though, while Jesse watched grinning,

wanting to embrace the wicked little donkey, Belshazzar's teeth closed on something else, something hard. Belshazzar did not know what it was. All the same he crunched down, as he always did when eating hay.

Suddenly the cartload of hay exploded! Hay flew in all directions as a man jumped out, knife in hand. Blood flowed down his ankle—the hard thing the white donkey had crunched!

Jesse shrank terrified against the wall of the commander's house as the stranger leaped from the cart. But Belshazzar swiftly moved to one side in surprise as the stranger leaped at him, hacking with his gleaming blade. It was the rider by night, the master of the black camel. Jesse knew him at once by his dark burnoose, the hooded cloak the people of the desert wore. It covered all of his face, all but his eyes, and these, Jesse saw, were a ferocious light green—the eyes of the red-bearded man at the Joppa Gate. The mysterious rider and the green-eyed inquirer after the family from Nazareth were one and the same!

Belshazzar needed no help against his attacker and went into swift action, easily dodging the knife. He'd fought other donkeys for so long that he was expert at dodging. He snaked back his ears and skinned back his lips. Instantly he whirled and lashed out with his hooves, almost catching the man in the chest. Then, having kicked, Belshazzar used his other weapons, his strong terrible teeth. He darted forward and grabbed at the man's arm, the arm that held the knife. The donkey's teeth missed the arm, but they buried themselves in the sleeve of the burnoose. The man cursed and the knife flashed coldly but missed its mark, the donkey's side. Belshazzar hung on grimly, but suddenly and unluckily the soft cloth ripped, giving way in Belshazzar's teeth.

The green-eyed stranger made a run for it, limping because of his bitten foot, and dashed into the thickening mists while an angry donkey followed, spitting out the cloth as he ran. Jesse, who was now able to move again, pounded at the donkey's heels. The stranger reached the high brick wall, dropped his knife to use both hands, and began to climb up the uneven bricking, going up it like a sand lizard. The donkey shot forward and snapped at the man's sandals, but the stranger was too high already and in another instant had dropped down on the other side of the wall.

Belshazzar felt he had won a battle. He lifted his head and brayed as loudly as he could. He brayed again and again in triumph. "Hee-haw! Hee-haw!" rang out into the damp air of Ashkelon as Jesse ben Abdiel stooped to pick up the piece of dark cloth and the knife. He knew at once what it all meant. The red-bearded man was an assassin, someone sent from King Herod to kill the carpenter's son wherever the carpenter might be. Herod did not intend to leave even one small male Israelite child alive. He would try to track them down and murder them all—even children who were protected by Romans in cities where Herod supposedly had no power.

XI. THE DANCER

Still holding the knife and the cloth ripped from the assassin's burnoose, Jesse stood as Romans boiled out of the garrison and out of the commander's house. The sentries, who had neither heard the silent fight nor seen it in the swirling sea mists, came running up to the boy and donkey now, naked swords in hand. Even the Roman commander, a clean-shaven man in a white purple-bordered toga, came out to see what all the commotion was about. He looked at the boy and donkey in great distaste.

And still Belshazzar brayed thunderously, cele-

174

brating his victory, attracting more and more attention. The Roman commander gestured to Jesse. The
boy knew what he meant, but he also knew he could
not stop the donkey once he had begun to bray his
victory bray. A soldier got behind Belshazzar and
tried to push him toward the stables while a second
Roman pulled. Belshazzar would not budge.

And then more people came—the carpenter, his
wife and baby, Saphir and one more important person, a dark-haired, white-faced little girl, who was
carried by the German slave woman. She lay back
limply in the big woman's embrace, wrapped in a
green gold-embroidered cloak, her feet dangling
down in the little red sandals only highborn Romans
were permitted to wear. At last Jesse ben Abdiel
saw Tullia, daughter of Marcus Tullius, governor
of Egypt.

The girl looked at him and smiled slightly, remembering his shepherd's pipes, but she laughed openly
at the foolish braying donkey. How amusing the
white animal was! The little girl's laughing words,
whatever they were, were drowned out by a barked
order from the Roman commander, and Jesse, to
his horror, saw one of the sentries move forward,
his sword held ready. The Romans were going to
kill Belshazzar because he could not be silenced
any other way. Bravely the boy moved toward the
man with the sword, but the second Roman drew
his sword too and gazed sternly at the boy, who held

the assassin's knife. Romans did not look with favor upon non-Romans who carried weapons and held them ready to use.

Jesse ben Abdiel let the dagger clatter onto the cobblestones of the courtyard. He ran unarmed to where Belshazzar stood with his head thrown back, still braying, and touched the white donkey on his right flank. There was only one thing the desperate boy could think of that would make the donkey stop his noise and keep him safe. If only Jesse could get Belshazzar to dance. But could the old donkey dance at all? It had been so long since he'd tried, and then he'd scarcely been able to lift up his hooves.

But something wonderful happened. A moment after he felt his former master's nudge, the donkey brayed his last "Hee-haw!" Then as the Romans looked on, he raised first his left front foot and then his right. Belshazzar hesitated now, then suddenly turned himself in a half-circle so he could look at the carpenter's wife and baby. Then, as Jesse frantically gave him his signals, the white donkey danced. At once the boy sensed that Belshazzar did not dance for the Romans or for Tullia or Saphir—or really even for him, although he gave the proper nudges. No, he danced for the people from Nazareth—for the baby, who kept solemn round eyes on him, and for the woman, who held out her hand palm upward when the animal's stiff old hind legs seemed as if they would not hold him when he rose up on them.

Belshazzar danced in Ashkelon as he had never danced in Israel. At the end of his performance he sank to his knees as he had always done in his final bow, but this time he bowed more deeply than ever before—to the baby and to his mother, to no one else, not to the carpenter who stood beside them, and certainly not to the Roman commander. Not for one instant had Belshazzar's eyes left the pair from Nazareth, the mother and the child.

Tullia, though, believed the donkey had danced for her. She clapped her hands and called out gleefully to Saphir. Jesse guessed at her Latin words— how "wondrous" the little dancing donkey was! Even the grim-faced Roman commander was smiling, and he motioned for the sentries to sheathe their swords and go back to their posts. The Romans appreciated a good show, and Jesse ben Abdiel thought suddenly of Nabal's words to Saul: "Never give a free performance." This one had not brought Jesse or Belshazzar any flung coins, but it had surely saved the donkey's life.

Now the Romans, the family from Nazareth and the crowd of slaves and soldiers left. The cold night mists of Ashkelon were not pleasant. They soaked through a person's clothing into his very bones. Only Saphir remained behind with Jesse.

"That was truly wonderful," the slave woman told the boy. "My mistress was pleased with your pipes —but not half so delighted as she was with the carpenter's donkey. How did you ever know he was a dancing donkey?"

Jesse only looked at her and shook his head. Then he put his arm about Belshazzar's neck, hoping she would understand.

"He was your donkey at one time? I have seen how you look at him sometimes." Saphir had a strange way of guessing things. "And that is why you travel with the carpenter—to be with this donkey?"

This time Jesse nodded.

Saphir bent down and picked up the knife Jesse had thrown onto the cobbles of the courtyard. She, like the others, had thought it was Jesse's knife. Every man in Israel carried one, and it was only an ordinary dagger. She gave it to Jesse, who drew back and waved it away with his hand. Then he showed her the piece of cloth he'd stuffed into his belt before he'd made Belshazzar dance.

"The knife is *not* yours?" the woman asked in surprise.

Jesse ben Abdiel drew out his own dagger and showed it to her. With it he slashed at the torn cloth and then pointed to Belshazzar. Finally he opened his mouth, pointing to his own teeth and finally to Belshazzar once more.

The quick-witted woman asked, "What is it? What has happened, Jesse?"

There in the mists Jesse reenacted what had taken

place in the courtyard earlier that evening. He
played both parts, the assassin's and Belshazzar's,
running back and forth desperately while the woman
watched with troubled eyes.

"Someone came here and hid in the garrison's hay
cart and then went over the wall and escaped? Is
that it, Jesse?"

Again and again the boy nodded. She had caught
his meaning. Saphir put her hand on his arm. "You
must show the Roman commander, too," she told
him. "I will bring him here and I will bring papyrus,
ink and a reed. I know how well you draw pictures.
He will not know any Hebrew words you know, but
Gaius Flavius will get the meaning of pictures you
make."

Jesse waited nervously, not liking the thought of
dealing further with Romans, but there was no help
for it. He looked over his shoulder at Belshazzar,
who had taken up his vigil again before the side
door as if nothing unusual had ever taken place.

The woman soon came back with the commander,
flanked by two slaves bearing torches. A little slave
boy followed her with reed, papyrus and ink. Jesse
had never used such things before, but he had seen
them used by scribes and rabbis, so now he sat down
on a bench and began to draw—first the black camel,
then the family from Nazareth, himself, and Belshazzar last, all traveling along a road. Next he drew
himself and the others sleeping while the tall camel

and rider passed. Finally he sketched a walled-in square filled with birds. While he drew, Saphir explained in Latin to the Roman, who had already examined the knife and cloth carefully. She told Gaius Flavius what Jesse meant, and then she had the boy act out for him exactly what he had shown her.

The commander's jaw was hard by the red glare of the torch. He spoke to the woman, and Jesse caught the name "Marcus Tullius" and "Tullia."

Saphir now shook her head violently and spoke to him again for some minutes. Gaius Flavius sent one of the slaves toward the garrison. The slave came back with a dozen fully armed legionaries, who stationed themselves around the courtyard. The Roman looked keenly at Jesse ben Abdiel, and to the boy's amazement he let his hand rest hard on his shoulder for a moment. The Roman *approved* of him! Then the commander strode off for his house.

Saphir and the torch-bearing slaves stayed with the boy. The woman was smiling. "Gaius Flavius says you are a lad of courage and intelligence. He knows you do not want to come inside his house. He says for you and that very valuable animal to remain here in the courtyard, then, to help guard the baby from Israel, who stays in this house. He says that it seems the donkey is a better watchdog than any of his greyhounds. He believed at first that someone from this city attacked the daughter of

Marcus Tullius, although he could not understand why. Then, I told him the truth—about the infant and about Herod. He has heard that story by now, of course. He knows the knife came from Israel and the cloth was woven there. I have told him that. He is going to order more legionaries to the ship in the harbor to keep it well guarded tonight and until we sail. He will send this news to Egypt and to Rome—and to Israel. This is another insult to Rome. Herod may know the full weight of Rome's anger because of this."

Saphir took the cloth and the knife from Jesse. "I will tell the carpenter the tale you have told Gaius Flavius," she promised. "Now, guard the baby well—that very remarkable baby. Do you not know who *he* is?"

Jesse looked at her, not understanding what she had said to him. There had been a question in her eyes, one she'd expected to have answered, but then she sighed and gently touched the boy's arm. "I forget, Jesse. You are almost grown, aren't you— near to thirteen, I am sure. It's not easy for a man of Israel to believe any more. Peace be with you." And Saphir, too, was gone into the house.

Jesse ben Abdiel went slowly back to the stoop, where the white donkey waited. He seated himself again and began to think once more. What would he do now that the carpenter and his wife and child were going to Egypt? Where would he go? A sudden hopeful thought came to him as he shivered in the chill. What if what Saphir had said on the road to Ashkelon was true—that he could earn money by playing his shepherd's pipes? Perhaps he could be a musician, and someday perhaps even a scribe? He would like to be a scribe in Jerusalem. His hopes began to rise as he gazed at Belshazzar, who looked, unwinking, at the door. The sight of the donkey drove Jesse's thoughts of the future, his own future, from his mind. How hard it would be to leave the donkey! But he knew that he must. If only Belshazzar would show some love to him!

Why, oh why, did the donkey always arrange to stand where he could see the woman and baby from Nazareth? Belshazzar never followed the carpenter with his eyes—only the other two. When the donkey gazed at them, he seemed to gain new strength. But that could not be! How could Belshazzar grow stronger just by *looking* at people? Yet Jesse felt this is what the donkey had done when he danced here in the courtyard, and the boy remembered how Belshazzar had made a circle to face the woman and child.

As Jesse turned these mysteries over in his mind, the tall carpenter opened the door and came out. He carried his brown robe over his arm, and he put it over the boy's thin shoulders on top of Jesse's own robe and his father's. The warmth was wonderful. "The woman, Saphir, tells me what happened in this courtyard before you made our donkey dance."

Jesse nodded, grateful for the heavy robe, as the carpenter went on. "We thank you, Jesse," the big man said with a smile. "The white donkey is yours! We have always known that he once truly belonged to you. My wife saw you take him in the stable at Bethlehem, and she knew you took back only what you believed to be your own. We have some gold yet. We did not give quite all of the treasure the three strangers from the east gave us in Bethlehem to the temple in Jerusalem. We shall buy another donkey in Alexandria. This one is yours!"

Jesse looked up, astounded by man's words. *Belshazzar his!*

It was the carpenter's turn to nod his head now. "We have long known of Herod's assassin following us. We have seen him and his camel, too, but my wife and I have had no fear of him. The child who travels with us was never in a moment's true danger. He is under the protection of the Eternal, and until he fulfills his destiny, nothing can touch him. No one will harm him. If he could speak, he would tell you that he wishes you to have this white donkey. Do not fear to take him. The animal will grow to love you again, and he will not tire or soon again grow old. Think for a moment, Jesse ben Abdiel. Which of all of us does your donkey most love?"

The carpenter, exactly like Gaius Flavius, the

Roman commander, put his hand on the boy's shoulder and went away to join the woman and child.

Belshazzar was his! Jesse was flooded with a golden joy at this news. But how oddly the gift had been given to him. And what questions the man and the slave woman asked! Jesse pondered the tall man's question. Which member of the family from Nazareth did the donkey love best? Jesse's forehead creased with deep thought. It wasn't the carpenter Belshazzar's eyes followed—but was it the quiet woman with the beautiful singing voice? Belshazzar didn't gaze at her face. No, he never did that. It was the baby he looked at—only the baby. Yes, it was the baby whom the donkey most loved. The child was what Belshazzar's eyes always sought. The carpenter had no terror of Herod's murderers. He knew that the child was protected and always would be protected. What was so special about the carpenter's baby? Saphir's face rose before Jesse, asking him once more if he did not know *who* the baby was.

A night wind came up, and as Jesse kept his watch with the Roman guards, the mists evaporated. One by one, two by two, the famous doves of Ashkelon came back. They landed on Belshazzar's back, and he permitted them now. They strutted about at Jesse's feet eating the grain Belshazzar had let fall when the slave had fed him.

Jesse ben Abdiel looked at the white birds, thinking of the sacrificial doves in the temple. These were Philistine doves, but they were sacred birds in Israel, too. The mute boy thought regretfully of how he had failed to give an offering at the temple in Jerusalem. But the temple was so rich and large and frightening. The little synagogue back in Arad was far more to Jesse's liking!

For the first time in some months the boy thought of his home, Arad, and of his father, Abdiel. What would Abdiel have made of all this? Jesse asked himself. Then in a flash of light, of radiance so bright it illumined his whole body, the son of Abdiel knew. He knew exactly and very certainly *who* the baby was!

The carpenter's child was the Messiah—the long-promised King of Kings, the "man who was to come." And he, Jesse, a poor mute boy, and Belshazzar, a humble old donkey, had traveled with the Messiah.

Jesse swelled with pride as he looked at his donkey, his heroic donkey from Israel, who had routed Herod's green-eyed assassin. Even dumb animals guarded the Messiah. Nothing would ever happen to harm *him* until *he* had accomplished the will of the Eternal. This the boy knew. In Egypt the baby would be safe. Herod had failed.

Jesse grinned at Belshazzar, his donkey. Now the mute boy knew that all would go well with him and his donkey too. Belshazzar would not age for years.

The carpenter had promised that, and Jesse knew that he had never given the donkey a tonic or potion. Belshazzar had drawn his strength only from the child he carried on his back.

Jesse dreamed great dreams in the night of Ashkelon, and he believed them. He would go home to Israel after he had made his farewells to Saphir and the carpenter and his family. He would enter the world of people and try once more. He would play his pipes, and Belshazzar would dance. Jesse no longer feared that Nabal would hear of the dancing donkey and come to take Belshazzar back. The carpenter had given him to Jesse ben Abdiel, and no one would ever take Belshazzar from him again. The boy and the donkey would not starve. People would throw lepton after lepton to the clever boy and the clever donkey. Yes, Jesse decided, he would try again! The family from Nazareth, the strange and wonderful family, had not failed him. They had wanted him to travel with them, and they had been kind to him. Saphir had not failed him. Perhaps others would not fail him either. And what did it matter if a few people did? There were kind folk in the world after all. He would search for his friend, Saul. Jesse believed that he'd find him and they would travel the roads of Israel together.

The mute boy dreamed magnificently. He would become a scribe in Jerusalem if he chose to. He would find a teacher someday, and he would be a scribe. All things were possible. If the child could make Belshazzar young and strong again, perhaps someday, when the baby was older, Jesse would let *him* know the story of his muteness and so *he* would know that Jesse had not been born speechless. But the son of Abdiel was in no hurry. No matter what happened, the true Messiah would return to Israel to fulfill what the prophets had said of *him* for hundreds of years. *His* destiny lay in Israel. *He* would come to Jerusalem when he was a man. Jesse ben Abdiel would watch for *him*. He would believe in *him*, and when he could write well enough he would tell others to believe that the "man who is to come" had come indeed! The boy recalled his father's words to him, true words, about the Messiah.

"You will know *him*, my son."

And Jesse did.

The boy took out his shepherd's pipes and put them to his lips. He began to play a joyous tune, one so lilting that he surprised even himself. As he played he watched his donkey, his Belshazzar, lie down for the night beside the door. He did not see the grim-faced Roman guards spaced around the courtyard at intervals glance at one another and smile and shrug to hear the strange speechless boy from Israel play such a happy melody in the somber damp night of Ashkelon.

AUTHORS' NOTE

Throughout this book we have tried to present as faithful a picture as we could of the world into which Jesus Christ was born. This search for accuracy, in an area in which Biblical scholars violently disagree, has by no means been an easy one. We have read the New Testament carefully, have looked at many maps of the ancient world in various university libraries, have pestered scholars and rabbis asking "peculiar" questions, many of them unanswerable, and have in general taken our information from whatever reputable source we could find. Three

books, however, have stood out as major aids. The
Bible, of course, is first. Then come *Ancient Israel* by
Roland de Vaux and *Daily Life in the Time of Jesus*
by Henri Daniel Rops.

KING HEROD AND CAESAR AUGUSTUS

The political situation at the time of Christ's birth
was, to say the least, a very confused one. Herod
the Great, a Hellenized, or Greek-favoring, Jew, was
king in name only. Rome and Caesar Augustus truly
ruled Israel. Herod, who spoke Greek in preference
to the language of Israel, was despised and hated
by his people, and he returned the compliment by
loathing them. The victim of a persecution complex,
he maintained an actual secret police of his own,
and it is true that the king sometimes walked about
anonymously, asking folk what they thought of him.
To his credit, however, Herod was personally
courageous, as witnessed by his willingness to come
out among his people, and a magnificent builder—
the builder of the great temple as well as theaters,
amphitheaters and hippodromes. He "got along"
with the Romans sent out to Israel and thereby saved
his land from the bloody rebellions it had known in
the past and would know again after his death—the
revolts that led to the final destruction of his temple.

We have depicted Romans as they were in Christ's
day—stern conquerors. The legionaries in Palestine

were chiefly Spaniards, Germans and Gauls, men who were told to humor the odd faith of the people of Israel. Jewish men were not required to give military service, and it is accurate that no Jew, unless he chose it himself, could be held in slavery for more than six years. The people of Israel were permitted their own coinage, also. Nevertheless, the Romans did not understand the Jews, nor the Jews the Romans. The Romans wrongly believed the Jews worshiped a pig's head. They thought this was why no Israelite would eat pork. They also wrongly suspected the Israelites of the practice of human sacrifice. On the other hand, the Jews were convinced that the Romans were impious heathens and felt that entering a Roman house would contaminate them. The wealthier people of Jerusalem, however, favored Roman rule, which kept the peace. It was the common folk who most disliked the conquerors from across the Mediterranean.

The Roman Empire was already vast in Herod's day. It embraced many lands, and people from these lands came as traders to Israel—Babylonians, Persians, Phoenicians, Egyptians and Anatolians. Generally these strangers could be told by their different styles of clothing as well as by their speech. The great gates of Jerusalem saw many folk who owed allegiance to Rome pass through their portals.

Many tongues were heard in Israel. Aramaic was the language Jesus spoke, although we know he read

Hebrew. Oddly enough, Hebrew has changed so little that Christ probably could read a twentieth-century Tel Aviv or Jerusalem newspaper. Latin was the speech of Rome, but it was not the common language or trading language. That seems to have been Greek. Numbers of Greek merchants lived in Jerusalem and in the Roman resort towns on the Sea of Galilee, such as Tiberias. Predominantly Greek cities were Hippos, Pella, Philadelphia and Gerasa.

Jews did not live only in the Holy Land in Christ's day. They were scattered throughout the Mediterranean world—in northern Africa, Syria, Tarsus, Macedonia, Greece and Babylon, and in Rome itself, where they were traders and protected by Caesar Augustus. The largest Jewish colony of all was in Alexandria, a city in the delta of the Nile River in Egypt. The Jewish population of Alexandria has been estimated to have been over a million—far larger than the population of Jerusalem in the first century B.C., as large as Rome. The population of Jerusalem has been estimated at about 150,000.

We have described Ashkelon, the port city, as archaeologists and Roman writers describe it. It is a fact that the city swarmed with white doves, which could not be killed without deeply offending the city goddess. The Philistines were non-Semitic, and it is true that the people of Ashkelon used more wood in their buildings than the people of Israel.

THE GREAT TEMPLE AND JERUSALEM

Our description of ancient Jerusalem is an accurate one. The city tended toward the guild system in Christ's day—the various city squares devoted to individual occupations did exist. So did the Antonia, the four-towered Roman garrison and the different city gates. We have tried to show how crowded and cramped the "city of the high place" was, and how very noisy.

As for the temple, it was begun by Herod in 20 B.C. on the site of King Solomon's old temple. It was still being built when Jesse ben Abdiel visited it and was not finished until about 63 A.D. Then, in 71 A.D., it was destroyed by Vespasian, the Roman emperor of that day.

Herod's temple was almost one of the wonders of the ancient world. We have described only two or three of its many glories. For example, it had nine gates, columns thirty-six feet high in the Court of Gentiles, a great altar, a Court of Men, a Court of Priests, a special hall where the judges of Israel sat, a sanctuary, and, of course, the huge bronze Nicanor Gate—which did take twenty men to open. The Court of Gentiles was, indeed, crowded with dove sellers, money changers, and bleating animals destined for the sacrificial altar. It was very likely a place of exciting but frightening turmoil to country folk.

Twenty thousand priests, divided into twenty-four classes, served in the temple. The Doctors of the Law were a special group, and they did teach in the temple courts. They would dispute points of the Law with any man who came to them. One of the most famous of these theologians was Hillel, who died ten years after Christ was born. Hillel's celebrated grandson, Gamaliel, could easily have been one of the body of scholars the young Christ confounded by his cleverness when he was a boy.

THE MESSIAH

The word Yahweh, or Jehovah, was not spoken aloud in ancient Israel. Instead, people referred to God as "The Merciful" or "The Eternal." "May heaven bless you," "May heaven be with you" and "Peace be with you" were common greetings of the day.

Although men and women did not use the actual name of God, they spoke openly of the Messiah and called him "the man who is to come." Zechariah, the Old Testament prophet, had said five hundred years before Christ's birth that the Messiah was to appear, but the more worldly and more wealthy people of Israel had abandoned hope. Not so the common people, women and children, although they had seen false Messiahs come and go many times in their land.

Those who waited for his coming believed that he would be born of the house of David and would be called either Yeshua or Emmanuel. They disagreed, however, about the sort of man he would be. Some thought he would be a sacrifice, a mournful man who took on himself the griefs, sins and sorrows of others. Others believed, or hoped, that he would be an invincible warrior who would drive the Romans and other heathen foreigners out of Israel.

CIRCUSES AND ANIMALS

Actually we do not know that there were traveling circuses in ancient Israel, but we rather suppose there were such things—probably very humble ones much like Nabal's. Acrobats, animal trainers and jugglers did exist in the ancient world. Horse racing was a favorite pastime of the Romans and was copied by the peoples they conquered, as were wrestling and boxing. Ropedancing is a very old art, too—perhaps as old as dice throwing. The sheep of Israel were commonly believed to dance to the lilt of their shepherd's pipes, and from sheep it's not much of a step to a dancing donkey. Dancing bears and donkeys today are standard animal acts. It is unlikely that they did not exist in the time of Herod.

Israel, for all that it was a rather barren land, teemed with animals. Only the Romans rode horses, and camels were used chiefly in caravans. The mule and the donkey were the chief transportation beasts. Israelites actually tied a foxtail or a red rag to a donkey's bridle between its eyes to keep it from falling.

There were many fish in the Sea of Galilee, and in the ponds of rich men there were carp. Water animals were the hippopotamus and crocodile. Judean shepherds feared the attacks of such beasts as wolves, lions, leopards, lynxes, bears, jackals and hyenas. It took much courage to be a shepherd. Other wild beasts were boars, antelopes, and foxes. Tob, the dog, is an unusual animal for our Jesse to love, but Jesse is an unusual boy. The dog was not generally a favored beast. In the time of Jesus, dogs were usually half wild and existed chiefly by scavenging. The poisonous asp and horned viper were feared serpents, while the white dove, crow and ibis were not uncommon birds. As can be expected in a time that did not know DDT and not too much about some forms of sanitation—although the Jews were a very clean, a ritually clean people—Israel abounded with insects: flies, wasps, mosquitoes, fleas, scorpions, centipedes, beetles and lice. One insect, the locust, was not only a pest but a food.

The people of the ancient Holy Land raised several kinds of domestic animals. They had oxen, cattle and goats as well as donkeys and fat-tailed sheep. In their towns and courtyards they kept ducks, pigeons, geese and other poultry.

Agriculture played such an important part in the life of Israel at Christ's time that some of the better-known first names derive from it. Rhoda means "rose," Susannah "lily." Rachel is "sheep" and Deborah "bee," while Tamar is "palm tree." Caleb means "dog," Nabash "serpent." The names of each person in this novel also have their meaning. Jesse means "gift," Saphir "beautiful," Jaala "wild she-goat"—and even more fittingly, "foolish" for Nabal.